DOMAINS OF DARKNESS

BY MARTYN RHYS VAUGHAN

NOVELS

The Stars Trilogy
Doom Of Stars
Resolution of Stars
Culmination of Stars

The Vampire Novels
No Truce With The Vampires: Those Who Sleep
No Truce With The Vampires: Those Who Wake

Hideous Night

NOVELLAS
Quantum Exile
The Cave of Shadows

SHORT STORIES
Domains of Darkness
Devouring Darkness

DOMAINS OF DARKNESS

Martyn Rhys Vaughan

These tales tell of strange happenings.

Would you read a book that foretells exactly what will happen on the remaining days of your life—including your death?

How would you react if you discovered that an alien race was colonising the Solar system and had some unspecified plan for the future of the human race?

What if you saw strange images in the shadows, images of creatures that did not have your best interests at heart? How could you convince people that you were not mad?

Read on, and discover how the people who had to actually deal with these problems reacted.

What would you have done?

Domains Of Darkness

Second Edition

COVER CREDITS

Cover Design by T C Evans (terry-evans.com)

The *hran* and planet Jupiter were digitally created, in part, using the MidJourney.com AI engine and Discord.com

The *Valveren* ships credits:
alfazetchronicles/123RF.com and
yourapechkin/123RF.com

EPIGRAPH

He rescued us from the domain of darkness…
Colossians 1:13

Yea, though I walk through the valley of the shadow
of death, I will fear no evil…
Psalm 23

Per ardua, ad astra. (Through Difficulty To The
Stars)
The motto of the Royal Air Force

Table of Contents

Martyn Rhys Vaughan

GERONTION

As usual for the time of year, the brilliant sun blazed unshielded in the harsh sky. The heat lay like a suffocating blanket over the yellow hills.

David stopped crumbling a clod of earth into fine dust with his toecap and yawned. He was vaguely aware that his grandfather had noticed that he hadn't been listening and was staring at him. David felt no remorse: he was bored with this strange trip, bored by his grandfather's promise of a wonderful revelation at the end of it if he would only be patient.

Patient! David snorted mentally; why were old men always telling him to be patient?

'Yes, Grandad, I was listening,' the boy lied, lifting his eyes to meet his grandfather's irritated gaze. For a moment, he almost felt sorry for the old man; he obviously enjoyed telling these cobwebbed tales of the old days, filled with all manner of unlikely happenings and fantasy. But he threw the feeling of empathy off and stared fixedly back at the man and it was his grandfather who looked away first. He suddenly looked very tired.

'You don't believe me, do you, David?' he said at last, his eyes turning to the parched ground. 'I'm trying to explain to you how things were in the old days. I know you find it hard to believe, but I was young once, and when I was a boy, things were different—I'm telling you!'

David half-succeeded in stifling a smile. He'd heard it all before from other members of the dwindling band of old-timers. Did it really matter how things had been in the dead past when those wrinkled creatures were as young and vital as he himself was? (if such a thing could be imagined). Did it matter if that slime-choked pool they had passed earlier had, in days gone by, been a wide, shining lake? It was a slime-choked pool now, and that was all that mattered. He reassured himself that this was probably the last time his grandfather would be making this pilgrimage: there obviously wasn't much life left in him.

Automatically and without noticing it, he brushed the descending sweat from his forehead. It was all so irrelevant to the urgent demands of modern living! He looked away from his slumped grandparent, away to the haze-shrouded vista of the northern horizon. There he was mildly surprised to see a greyish cloud rising wispily like a dusty cobweb above the scarred ramparts of the nearest hill.

'So many people,' the old man was muttering, 'so many; all busy with their little lives, going around making money, planning foreign holidays, moaning about the weather. The weather!'

This last observation seemed to afford him some grim amusement, for his cracked lips jerked spasmodically a few times. He turned and looked directly at David again.

'Well, I suppose you want to know why I dragged you up here into the hills,' he said, and there seemed to be a hint of a note of triumph behind the question, as if some grand revelation was about to be made manifest.

David shrugged to show his indifference, but something about his grandfather's look was puncturing his insouciance. There was a hungry expectancy in those pale eyes.

'I…'

The boy's sentence died. Something was wrong. There was a subtle change in the quality of the light beating down upon them, as if the midday had suddenly become evening.

He turned northward. The grey cloud he had noticed earlier had darkened into a powerful ebony shape, and no longer was it a thin veil: it was developing a billowing, castellated structure and was swelling visibly like a pool of black blood from some dying creature. A deep shadow was crawling across the tortured plateau towards them.

His grandfather spoke again, and somehow his voice had strengthened and become resonant like an Old Testament prophet declaiming the imminent destruction of Nineveh.

'It only happens at this time of year now, and only up here can you really feel it!'

He laughed, but with a slightly maniacal edge to the laughter.

The shadow passed over them, and David was shocked by the sudden drop in temperature. The shadow had been like some obscene bird of prey, swooping hungrily toward them.

'I want to go back down now, Grandad,' he said, keeping his voice slow and firm.

His grandfather did not look at him and shook his head impatiently. He was staring at the swelling cloud with a fierce expectancy.

'No, not yet,' he snapped. 'No, the best is still to come!'

David stood up: he had decided to leave this weird place. Down there in the valley there was normality; his mother, his brother, the girl he had chased last week and nearly caught; the chickens nesting in the flaking metal skeletons which old people said had once had the power to move by themselves.

'Well, I'm going,' he said quickly, 'I've had enough; mother will…'

He stopped. Something small and soft had hit the side of his head. Now really alarmed, he turned and looked in the direction of the blow but, even as he moved, it happened again. It took his spinning mind some moments to realise something strange and magical was happening.

'Grandad, Grandad!' he yelled, feeling a liquid coursing its way over his cheeks to his bewildered lips. 'Water—water is falling from the sky!'

'Now do you believe me!' the old man cried, raising his arms as the drops came thicker and faster, punching little craters in the dust.

David too felt an exhilaration rising, and went to his grandfather's side and held his withered arm, almost tenderly.

'I'm sorry, Grandad,' he whispered, 'how was I to know?'

And so they stood there, the old man and the boy, neither really knowing of the terrible discovery that had been made in the forgotten twentieth century, of how the world leaders had been warned of the possibility of a runaway greenhouse effect due to humanity's stupidity and how they had not done enough to curb the gases flooding the atmosphere. And how in the middle of the following century, the climatic zones had suddenly shifted, deflecting the weather patterns that people had relied on, and making parts of their planet uninhabitable.

And so they stood there together in the first warm drops of the British Rainy Season, looking out over the splintered ochre hills, as the January winds whipped the fading cloud into tatters above the bald peaks of old Blencathra.

ZERO AS A LIMIT

I became aware my boss was standing behind me. I could feel his eyes drilling into me like a gimlet slowly being screwed into my skull. How I knew he was there, I don't know. I don't believe in psychic powers, but somehow, I knew. I hesitated before acknowledging him, looking at my screen with theatrical attention, but I knew I couldn't drag it out for long. So I swivelled the standard-issue office chair and reluctantly looked him in the eye. Somehow, I always thought I would see red, blazing demon eyes but no, they were the usual dim, grey orbs I had seen so often. Looking into them was like looking into a cobwebbed cellar from the top of a very high flight of steps.

'Kowalski,' he said, in a voice as flat and grey as his gaze, 'My office. Now.'

I caught the glances of my colleagues as I rose slowly. They were glances of pity, tinged with relief that Schwartz had not descended on them like a vulture onto a ripe carcass.

Schwartz's room was small but full of books from floor to ceiling. Five computer monitors were permanently on, displaying the results of complex equations in real-time. I was frightened of Schwartz; he knew more about my job than I did. Moreover, he held two first-rank PhDs in which complex analysis and tensor calculus played important parts:

both great oceans in which I had barely dipped a toe in.

The grey eyes bored into me, holding me in an immaterial vice.

'Your work, Kowalski,' he finally said in colourless tones, much as a Spanish inquisitor might have begun his investigation into the latest heresy, 'is inadequate.'

There it was. The dread word. The word that conveyed that the *auto da fé* was approaching. The black cap word. Inadequate. There was no appeal.

Or was there? I was tired. I didn't really want this job. Or any other job. I just wanted my dead family back: the four of us sitting together, looking out over the lake with the light winds of the afternoon rippling its surface.

Suddenly I didn't care. The heretic would snatch the instruments of torture and turn them on his tormentor.

'And why is that, Dr Schwartz?' I said coldly. But even then, I couldn't drop his title.

He showed no sign of surprise or irritation at my defiant tone. He was the total professional, as usual. His hand indicated the nearest monitor.

'You set 2029 as your Base Year and failed to seasonally adjust. 2035 was the correct year as the phenomenon was by then being accurately reported.'

I felt my courage grow. What did it matter now? I was sacked, for certain sure. So what did any of it matter anymore?

'2029 was the year in which all the authorities agree that the phenomenon began. As for seasonal adjustment, there is absolutely no evidence that seasonality played any part in its development. The tests I ran gave p values that indicated that the null hypothesis was equally valid in any interpretation of the early stages.'

Did I see a flicker of surprise then—as if a gardener had been taken aback by the worm under his spade finally turning?

'Everyone—apart from you apparently—knows that p values depend upon initial assumptions. Were your initial probabilities Classical or Bayesian?'

'Bayesian,' I returned swiftly, 'the prior probabilities were subject to Peer Review, and I stand by them.'

I felt a hot wave rise from my abdomen into my extremities. I was going down now, I knew, but Schwartz would remember that I had stood there in his office and bested him.

But, of course, I had underestimated him. Well-manicured fingers pushed a sheet of paper towards me. The flat voice came again; unperturbed, indifferent, disinterested, god-like.

'Your calculations for sampling error, I believe.'

I looked at the figures, wary, alert, like a mink testing the entrance of a trap.

'Yes,' I said; because it was all I could say.

'Line 3, Mr Kowalski, Line 3.'

I felt a thin layer of greasy sweat suddenly form on my forehead.

Line 3, Line 3. Oh no, Oh God No!

The decimal point was displaced. The sampling errors were ten times too small!

It was all over; Schwartz had won again. I actually felt my head dip as I accepted defeat.

But he had not finished with me—just as a cat will continue to toy with a dying bird. The second monitor was turned to me, glowing with the putrid green of dissolution.

'Your curve of decay,' he said, each word given the same amount of stress, making him sound like a Twentieth Century speech delivery program, 'you used an asymptotic curve. As any infant knows on his first day in nursery, an asymptotic curve does not reach the abscissa except at infinity.'

Suddenly a red fury surged through me. *Take him down, take him down!* a voice in my head screamed. I stood up, suddenly towering over him, (for he was a short man), 'I used an asymptote deliberately!' My voice had become a scream. 'To give all those thousands of survivors a scrap of hope. The asymptote does not reach zero. But that's not the real fit to the data—we both know that! The real curve will hit zero in five years' time. Five years and the mutant superflu that broke out in 2029 will have killed everyone on the planet and the population will reach zero. Not at infinity—five bloody years! That's why I didn't use the real curve!'

I spun around and left his office. I could spend my last days sitting by the lake, thinking about my wife and children.

But I glanced back at Schwartz just as the main door closed.

Schwartz had also been a family man.

He was crying.

For his lost family.

CIRCLES

Johnson had known nothing of the Circles of Hell that night as he hurried back to his flat that stormy evening, eager to relax with his new adult movie. So how was he to know that there are witches out there and that he was about to meet a real, live one? He had always thought that they were just silly fantasies in video games for dull, retarded children. Certainly, that was what was in his subconscious when the rag-wearing hag jumped out in front of him.

'Spare some coppers for an old lady', the hideous wretch whined. 'I ain't eaten since last Thursday. Spare a few coppers, and I'll bring you luck.'

Johnson glared and flicked the butt of his last cigarette at her, narrowly missing an eye.

'Out of my bloody way, you old bitch,' he snapped and began to push past her.

'Please, sir,' the crone pleaded, 'Just a few coppers.'

Johnson wasn't quite sure why he did it, but he pushed her away so violently that she bounced off the nearby wall and fell at his feet like a pile of discarded rags. He glanced around to see if the scene had been witnessed, wondering if he should stop and at least apologise for the trickle of blood that was now making its way along the pavement, but the call of the adult movie was too strong and, anyway, people like this old woman were simply too damn ugly to make it worth his while.

He had just taken one step onward when he felt a bony hand on his shoulder. He spun around to face the withered creature.

'You are cursed!' the old woman hissed, her hideous features made more hideous by burning hatred. 'Madame Agatha curses you to be dragged to the Fifth Circle of Hell!'

Johnson found himself strangely shocked by this display of rage but decided that this was no time to display weakness.

'Crawl back under your stone you *<Expletive Deleted>* bag of*<Expletive Deleted>*. I'm a very important guy and people like you should be put in a bag and drowned!'

The old woman did not appear to be listening and continued: 'Before midnight tomorrow you will see a ring, and then a Fire Demon will appear and drag you to the Fifth Circle. Madame Agatha never lies!'

Johnson was about to deliver another withering insult when something happened that turned him rigid with eye-popping fear. There had been a small puff of violet smoke, and a blood-red little imp had appeared on Madame Agatha's left shoulder. Another violet puff and a snot-green imp materialised on the other shoulder. Both imps leered horribly at Johnson.

He ran all the way home.

And so, after a nightmare-filled night, he faced the fateful day converted into a firm believer in the occult and witches in general, and in Madame Agatha in particular.

But it all seemed so simple—all he had to do was avoid seeing some sort of a ring before midnight that day. Avoid it until the witching hour, and then he could decorate his flat with Olympic flags if he wanted to (or Madame Agatha's guts, his mind added vengefully).

First of all, he had to stay all day indoors. If he went outside, his first glimpse of a car or a bicycle or a pizza would damn him. (Literally.)

'Stay in all day,' he thought, over and over, 'Do not look at anything that could be interpreted as a ring.'

He looked around the flat through narrowed eyelids. What circular objects were there that he could accidentally see? His clock was OK; it was digital. He didn't own any LPs or CDs. His table was rectangular, as was the mirror on the wall. He decided to have his reflection give him a reassuring grin and was halfway to the mirror when it hit him—his eyes!—if he saw his own pupils, they would be circular and damn him! He approached the mirror from the side and turned its reflecting side to the wall. He wiped his forehead, conscious that his close escape had caused blobs of cold sweat to pop out of his clammy skin. He sat down heavily, looking furtively around, desperately trying to think of other circular traps waiting for him. Then, turning his head, he noticed a shaft of golden sunlight illuminating the floor near his main window. Ah, to see the sweet sky again, Johnson thought, that would calm his nerves.

He was almost at the window when once again he realised his folly—he'd done it again! If he saw the sun, it would be the end; even if it were behind clouds, there were such things as haloes.

Traps everywhere! But then a steely determination came over him. He would beat Madame Agatha and then strangle her with one of her own filthy rags!

Johnson closed the blinds and sat back down, breathing heavily. He was confident there was nothing even vaguely circular in the flat. All he had to do was sit it out.

The hours crawled by, each one feeling like a century. He had no appetite for a meal but nibbled some dry crackers—rectangular, of course. As midnight approached, the strain on his nerves became intolerable. He paced back and forth like a wounded animal. He'd give anything for a drink. But, wait a minute!—had he finished that whisky? Was the bottle still in the drawer? He opened it. There was no whisky but, joy of joys, a cigarette packet! His heart sank as he snatched it out of the drawer—it felt empty—but no! There was one cigarette inside, and flat as a flatworm, so there was no chance of seeing the dreaded circle. He glanced at the clock—five minutes to midnight. He'd done it. He'd won!

'You messed with the wrong man this time, you *<Expletive Deleted>* bag of*<Expletive Deleted>*!' he shouted out loud. He felt the tension slowly fade away as he sat back down in his armchair. After a slight panic that the cigarette might be too flat to light, Johnson was gratified to see the end glow a cheerful red. He drew the comforting smoke deep into his lungs. It was bliss! And then, as he always did, he blew out a perfect smoke ring.

Madame Agatha wasn't always entirely accurate when it came to her curses. So, when the Fire

Demon appeared, it dragged Johnson to the Seventh Circle of Hell, not the Fifth.

Perhaps one day you'll meet him there.

IMPACT TRAJECTORY

Lieutenant-Commander Douglas Mitchell looked up from the viewer and saluted crisply as the Controller of Space Station Triton-1 walked in. The Controller, a plumpish, red-faced man with streaks of white invading his mousey hair, replied limply and leaned over the globe of the viewer.

In the viewer was a cruelly bright, gleaming star, standing out like a superb diamond on its bed of blackness. That star blazed brighter than had any star in the sky of Earth because it was a special star—it was Sol itself, home star of humanity. Also in the viewer were two crescent worlds—one vast and blue-green with wisps of white near its limb; the other much smaller and a dull white with wispy markings. They were mighty Neptune and its major satellite Triton.

'I wonder what they think of us down there on Earth, Mitchell,' the Controller said in a distant voice. 'Tucked up on their wreck of a planet with their goddam labour-saving machines, soft, sugary food and endless, mindless pap as entertainment.'

Mitchell raised his eyebrows.

'I beg your pardon, sir.'

The Controller gave something like a sigh. 'What's the point, Mitchell?' he rapped, turning slowly. 'Answer me that.'

'The point of what, sir?'

The Controller crossed to the huge crystal window and jabbed a finger at the maze of starfields. At an indeterminate distance away, a silvery, needle-like object hung, seemingly motionless against the stars.

'Interstellar probe Pholos,' he muttered, turning his ponderous form to gaze deep into the blackness. 'Here out by Neptune, I sometimes wonder if we can see life as it really is. Away from the artificialities of so-called civilisation, we can accept plain, simple facts.'

'I believe that one of those facts is the need for humanity to explore and understand the universe that we inhabit,' Mitchell replied, a little stiffly.

'Invasion is a better word, Mitchell,' snapped the Controller, suddenly angry. 'Understanding, hah!' It was a bitter, disillusioned laugh. 'Starving humanity's contamination of other worlds—those are the facts that I see. Why should the Directors back on Earth run our lives: Do This, Do That, Don't Do That! What do they know, sat there in their nice, cool offices looking down on the starving masses? Perhaps out here, we can see the true place of humankind in the universe.'

'Sir,' Mitchell began, hesitantly, 'perhaps out here with all your responsibilities, you're…'

The Controller gave him no time to finish.

'I'm what, Mitchell? Boy, I know your kind, fresh out of college with your stars still gleaming on your shoulders. No experience of life; never had to make a decision except what to order for your lunch! Come back in thirty years before you presume to make comments about me!'

Mitchell felt his face flush. He was all too aware of his inexperience, this being his first real assignment as Security Officer. The obvious signs of embarrassment on his face made him feel even more discomfited—which simply increased the flushing. He decided that this conversation with the Controller was getting a little dangerous, and he changed the subject.

'Sir, Pholos is leaving in five hours. Countdown is already underway.'

The Controller instantly looked more alert. He crossed to a nearby desk and flipped a toggle. 'This is the Controller: Report.'

A pleasant, asexual voice came on the line. It sounded quite human, although of indeterminate gender, but both men knew it was synthetically generated.

'We are at T minus five hours, thirty-seven minutes, two seconds, sir.'

The Controller flipped the toggle again, and seemed deep in thought as he gazed at his blurred reflection in his desk's surface. Finally, he glanced up.

'Anything else you want to tell me, Mitchell?'

Mitchell was determined not to lay himself open to any further criticism.

'Two objects from the Kuiper Belt have collided near the inner edge of the Belt. And the debris cloud is coming this way.'

'Any danger to this station or to the probe?'

'No sir—it should pass at a safe distance.'

'Then why bother to tell me?'

An awkward silence fell.

'Alright Mitchell, you can check off now. Report to launch control in five hours. Dismissed.'

Mitchell saluted, and as he left, he noticed that the Controller had hardly bothered to reply.

***

June Shaw was a slim, attractive redhead. She was also the Chief Physicist on the Pholos Project.

Mitchell drank in the lithe grace with which she sat opposite him in the quiet alcove of the Recreation Room, and wondered yet again how a woman could have won the Lottery in both looks and intelligence quite so spectacularly. She regarded him silently for a moment, the only sound being the faint grating of her spoon as it swirled her white coffee.

Dammit, thought Mitchell, *how can someone make stirring a cup of coffee look like an invitation to foreplay?* As he looked at her, he was aware of a faintly amused smile playing on her inviting lips.

'And what has happened to you?' she queried, her head on one side in mock puzzlement, 'that you should be so silent on such a momentous day? And,' she added mischievously, 'in the presence of so momentous a lady?'

Mitchell lifted his head with what seemed a great effort.

'It's the Controller, June. I'm worried about him. He's acting strangely about the Pholos project.'

Shaw nodded as if she had known this for a long time.

'It's not unknown. Some people—particularly men of a certain age—become somewhat paranoid when isolated from the normal Terrestrial environment. They can develop delusions of grandeur—or delusions of *adequacy*, in the case of our dear Controller.'

'How do you know this?' Mitchell demanded, a little shocked at the dismissive tone in which June spoke of his superior officer. 'I thought your qualifications were in subatomics, not psychology.'

She shrugged.

'It's common knowledge. Though you apparently hadn't heard of it. Are you sure you're cut out for a job in Security?'

Mitchell felt his face flushing again. This damn woman! If he could get her alone for a while, he'd show…

He pushed the sadomasochistic fantasy back into the subconscious from whence it had suddenly erupted. *Think cold thoughts*, he told himself, *don't look at her figure, her bosom. Think Cold.*

Cold as the snows of Triton, hundreds of kilometres below.

Cold.

'Paranoid?' he finally echoed, still wondering if Shaw had noticed his boyish flushing. 'What possible harm or danger could there be in Pholos? It's not a ridiculous faster-than-light battleship; just a plain-vanilla ion-drive probe to Proxima Centauri, one that'll take all of forty-five years to get there.'

Shaw laughed, a melodious laugh that sent shimmering red-copper hair tumbling over her shoulders. *God! Even in work clothes, she's stunning!* She looked at him from under long lashes.

'Maybe Pholos isn't entirely scientific.'

Mitchell looked at her sharply. Was this another of her games? If it wasn't, then as Security Officer, he couldn't let a remark like that pass.

But Shaw was no longer looking at him. Instead, she was staring down at her coffee and seemed fascinated by the spiralling swirl of froth on its surface.

'It always intrigues me when looking at bubbles like these; how much they resemble a galaxy.'

Mitchell grabbed her wrist suddenly, and she gave a little gasp of surprise.

'I'm Security Officer here—or have you taken over that job as well? What did you mean by that entirely-scientific crack?'

Shaw pulled her wrist away and stared at red marks discolouring the creamy flesh.

'That hurt.'

'I'm sorry—but for God's sake, stop talking in riddles. I thought we knew each other better than that.'

Shaw drained her coffee and looked out across the crowded Rec Room.

'Strange to look at all these people carrying on with their normal little lives. As if they were important. As if they mattered to the universe.'

'Are you going to tell me, or not?' growled Mitchell, his knuckles whitening as he gripped the table. 'Look, I've got an automatic in my jacket. Do you want me to take it out?'

Shaw laughed again, her brilliant emerald eyes gleaming with tolerant amusement.

'You really are too melodramatic, aren't you, Douglas?' She leaned forward until Mitchell could feel the faint whisper of her breath on his lips. 'But you're weak, Douglas, weak! Men are not men today, just women with slightly different soft bodies. Not like in the Twenty-first century. Men were men in those days!'

'The Twenty-first century?' Mitchell echoed bemusedly. 'Those days of terrorism, famine, hate? June, what is there to admire about that time?'

'Humanity was different then,' she snapped, her eyes suddenly blazing. 'Leaders took what they wanted—and to Hell with all in their way!' Her voice was a whiplash, steeled with bitterness, marinaded in contempt. Despite his need to be a detached professional, Mitchell recoiled slightly. It was as if he had opened an innocuous door and found a tiger behind it. The human tiger continued her tirade. 'Earth is now one big, happy family— and one helluva bore!'

Mitchell gasped—this was mad, insanely dangerous!

But Shaw seemed calmer as she reached into her purse and retrieved a long, thin white cylinder. Before Mitchell's puzzled eyes, she then took out a small metal object, clicked it and applied the resultant blue flame to one end of the cylinder. Mitchell suddenly remembered: now that all cancers were at the very least controllable, some of the intelligentsia had taken to smoking tobacco again. This habit at least was in character for someone who admired the past so totally. Calmly, she directed a curling, grey cloud at Mitchell and chuckled as he recoiled, coughing.

'So what are you going to do, Douglas? Arrest me for my opinions? Tie me up for uttering a harmless little speculation? No, you won't do any of that, Douglas, and I'll tell you why. Because you want me. But like all the other jellyfish on this station that call themselves men, you've done nothing about your need for me. Perhaps when you're alone in your cabin you play with yourself while sweating over a picture of me. But that's all you'll ever get, Mr Security Officer.' She rose suddenly from her seat and stood over him. It seemed to Mitchell's confused senses that she was somehow infinitely tall, a Pallas Athena leaping fully armed from the head of Zeus. 'I've had enough of this.' She started to walk away but, after a few steps, looked over her shoulder. 'And by the way—it's *Doctor* Shaw—not June.'

***

'T minus Fifty minutes,' announced the smooth, asexual voice.

The Controller slowly got to his feet as if every movement caused him pain. He remained still for a long time, his tired eyes roving over a cabin which tried to hide the fact that it was part of a space station by cheap imitations of current Terrestrial styles. As always, the large viewer showed Pholos still apparently motionless against the unwinking splendour of the stars.

He pressed a button, and from the cavity which appeared in the wall, he took out his best dress uniform and thoughtfully fingered the medal ribbons. He dressed slowly and deliberately and then with a last glance at the softly glowing viewer, he left the cabin and stepped into the elevator.

***

'What the hell?' snapped Dr June Shaw as, without her permission, her cabin door slid to one side, and Douglas Mitchell stepped in. 'What do you mean by following me?'

Mitchell ignored the question and sat, uninvited, on her bed.

'I think you know more than you're telling me, Doctor Shaw. I think there's something behind your tantalising little comment about Pholos not being entirely scientific. Now talk!'

Shaw responded with a laugh and leaned back, placing her arms behind her head.

'My, who's been reading the Security Manual? Are you trying to impress me?'

Mitchell's sarcastic rejoinder was never uttered. At that moment from the speaker in Shaw's room, and indeed, from every speaker throughout the station, came the Controller's voice, sounding flat and tired; so very, very tired.

'To all my colleagues on Space Station Triton-1, I have a very important message. You have been labouring under a cruel illusion: that you were working on a noble mission to advance humanity's understanding of the cosmos. In fact, you have been preparing for humanity's invasion of the stars; an invasion which will pollute other worlds with our filth and madness. I have thought about this long and hard, and I have come to a very important decision: I cannot permit that to happen. We have ruined one world; there will be no others.

'So I am sending a message to those madmen on Earth. I have altered Pholos's launch coordinates. The AIs have calculated the impact trajectory for me; one which send Pholos plunging into the Sun. When the fools on Earth have seen the destruction of their expensive folly, they will have to think again and abandon this wicked attempt to dominate the stars.

'Thank you for listening. I hope you are with me on this. This is the Controller, signing off.'

Mitchell turned to speak to Shaw but stopped in amazement—her face was white and contorted into a horrid mask of terror! She seemed to be in the midst of some seizure; he watched her hands making spasmodic clawing motions on the fabric of her chair.

Mitchell grabbed her and shook her small frame.

'What's the matter! June, June, speak to me!'

She shook him off and spoke flatly, ignoring him, staring at the door.

'Impact trajectory for the Sun. No, no, no!'

He held her again.

'What's so terrible? It's an incredible waste of resources; all the work the people here have done, and it means the end of that poor bastard's career. But no one's going to get hurt. Pholos hitting the Sun is less than a flea bite.'

Shaw, at last, turned to face him, her breath coming in great ragged gasps. Her eyes were wide and staring, like an animal caught in a trap.

'You don't understand, you dumb moron. The bomb! The bomb!'

'What bomb? What are you talking about?'

Shaw took control of herself; Mitchell was never to know what that effort had cost her, but he saw a steely look come into her face.

'No more subterfuge. I am a member of a group, an organisation, a coterie of elite scientists who know what is best for humanity. Some years ago, we made a breakthrough—we could create a dampening field that can disrupt the strong nuclear force.'

Mitchell frowned.

'Strong nuclear force—so what?'

Even in existential crisis she could not prevent a look of disdain play briefly over her features.

'*Strong nuclear force*, you stupid animal—it's the fundamental glue that holds the protons together in the nucleus. Remove that, and they fly apart, releasing their binding energy in a flash of the hardest radiation that this universe can sustain.'

'And the Controller's impact trajectory?'

'When the bomb goes off in the Sun, it'll set off a chain reaction. If the dampening field gets down to the core, it'll act like a subatomic prion and disrupt the proton-deuteron chain!'

With mad strength, Mitchell dragged the beautiful scientist to her feet and shook her like a doll.

'So why put it on the Pholos, you crazy fucking bitch!'

She did not resist the shaking, and her voice became detached as if she were addressing a room of adoring students.

'The equations are incredible. I've never seen anything like them. We can't quantify the detonation within anything smaller than an error bar of several orders of magnitude. With that level of uncertainty, we couldn't explode it anywhere near Earth. Instead, we were going to explode it when it was entering the Oort Cloud. Then reveal ourselves and make our demands. We want to rule Earth—not destroy it!'

Mitchell's mind whirled, and he felt a dreadful tsunami of insanity surging within his skull. In his training, he had heard reports, reports little more than rumours, of a secret organisation that was gradually infiltrating the highest levels of society; an organisation that knew exactly what it wanted: power—the power to mould the world to their ideal of human perfection. But the conclusion of those discussions had been that such an organisation belonged to the world of conspiracy theorists and fantasists. But unbidden, he suddenly remembered a line from a very old book he had read as a boy: "The Devil's greatest trick was to convince everyone that he did not exist." Evidently, there was a conspiracy—and a very successful one.

And very dangerous.

'And all the physicists aboard are part of your group?'

She nodded.

'All the important ones. The ones who just take orders and press buttons aren't ours.'

He shook her again—he had to know precisely what he was dealing with.

'And if the impact disrupts the Sun, as you suspect—what then?'

This time she pulled away and stood staring at him, her bosom heaving, features twisted into a mask of contempt.

'You damn, damn fool! How can anybody be so stupid? Our bomb is only five hundred grams of neutral matter—but if it disrupts the Sun, it'll create a bomb of Solar mass! The explosion will rip this galaxy apart and be visible out to the ends of the observable universe! You've got to change that impact trajectory!'

He struck her then, and, without waiting to see her fall, he ran out of the room.

Mitchell arrived at the door of the Control Room after calling for an essential tool to break through the door. A little cluster of technicians were standing in front of it in abject bewilderment. Obviously, nothing like this had ever happened in their quiet lives, but, come to think of it, Mitchell thought to himself—the same was true of him. One of the technicians rushed up to him, seeking some explanation as to why everything had suddenly changed.

'It's the Controller, sir,' the young man gasped, almost sobbing. 'He's gone mad or something. Ordered us all out at the point of an automatic!'

Another technician ran up.

'It's not his fault—he should have been relieved months ago—all this responsibility, the isolation! Don't hurt him, please!'

Mitchell looked at the visibly shaken technicians with a mixture of emotions; one of them, he noticed wonderingly, was a cold disdain. They were quite obviously terrified, but in fact, nothing had actually happened to them, as yet. And they were standing there with pale faces completely free of the crushing load that Mitchell now carried—the horrific understanding that everyone on Space Station Triton-1 was taking part in a drama so dire that it could end in a conflagration vast enough to tear down the foundations of the entire galaxy! He had to act to end this danger without revealing the full scale of the horror to people who were already in blind panic.

Perhaps Shaw had not been entirely wrong about the quality of modern men.

Mitchell spoke into his collar communicator, trying to keep the fear out of his own words. 'Where are those bloody burners?'

'Coming now, sir,' a tinny voice replied into his earpiece. Mitchell looked at the door. It was just a standard fitting—no one had ever intended the Control Room to withstand a siege—the burners would cut through in minutes.

And within the Control Room, the sole remaining technician was drumming her fingers nervously along the ebony-coloured metal of her control station, the flashing of various indicators sending coloured light and shadow dancing across her face.

'Sir,' she pleaded again, 'What's gotten into you? Put that thing down, please!'

The Controller smiled for an instant, but his lined face remained that of a stern parent.

'You don't understand, do you? It's not that thing itself,'—he gestured briefly at the silver dart of the Pholos framed in the viewer, 'it's what it stands for. Contamination, girl! Can't you see that! The real soul of life is out there, the eternal, indestructible universe which must be kept free from the grabbing paws of murderous mankind!' His eyes seemed to blaze, and the girl flinched as he waved the automatic around, apparently lost in his vision of an unsullied universe.

Just then, there was a flurry of yellow-white sparks, and a large section of the door fell inwards with a jarring crash. And a man was revealed, silhouetted against the brighter light of the corridor.

'Stay there!' the Controller roared. 'I'm not quite finished. Stay exactly where you are, or I promise I will kill you.'

Mitchell stopped. His eyes had not yet adjusted to the dimness of the room, but slowly he became aware of a bulky form with the glint of metal in its hand.

'Put it down, sir!'

The Controller fired. The beam of energy his automatic emitted was invisible, but the hole that appeared in the deck just in front of Mitchell's feet was not.

'One more step boy, and the next one will drill you an extra eye.'

'Sir, you don't understand. You must not activate the Pholos—therc's a bomb on board which could destroy everything!'

The Controller actually laughed.

'God, you must be desperate, boy! A bomb on board! How could that happen! Sounds like you'd better go back to college and start again. It won't wash. I'm not going to let humans spill out into the stars after the mess they've made of their world. I can hear the dying cries of all the helpless creatures that people like you drove into extinction through greed and cruelty. The commands have been set. There remains only one thing left to do.'

The Controller turned his back. Mitchell had a moment of indecision, but he knew what had to be done. He leapt forward, but as he did so, the Controller's automatic sent out its invisible energies again. But it was not Mitchell who was the target: the main control panel lit up with cascading fountains of eye-tearing blue and violet flame. Mitchell crashed into the Controller, and both men hit the floor hard. Despite his fleshy bulk, the older man was surprisingly strong, and Mitchell struggled to keep his balance as they swayed back and forth in a weird shuffling dance.

Then all of a sudden it stopped. The Controller abandoned his grasp of Mitchell and stepped back. Then, looking the younger man directly in the eye, he smiled; a calm, beatific smile. It looked as if years had suddenly tumbled from his face; it seemed to grow younger before Mitchell's astounded gaze.

'What am I fighting for?' the Controller said in a quiet voice; the voice of a man who has seen his labours come to fruition and knows that there is no more to do: knows that he may now depart in peace. 'It is finished. There will be no contamination.'

He stood to one side, revealing the tangled mass of smoking wreckage that had once been the main control panel. Mitchell almost collapsed then, his legs went weak and a terrible whirling sensation sent the Control Room spinning.

He understood: The Controller had sent the final command to send Pholos plunging into the warm heart of the Solar system and had destroyed the only mechanism which could have countermanded those orders.

Soon the engines would fire, and the terrible descent would begin. Nothing could stop it now. Mitchell steadied himself and removed the automatic from the Controller's unresisting hand.

'Sir,' he said quietly, 'you are under arrest.'

***

Mitchell slapped his fist against the cold metal of the console.

'Come on!' he bellowed at the terrified-looking technician in the viewer, 'There must be some way we can restore the telemetry link! What are we paying you for!'

'It's no use, Douglas,' a soft voice said behind him. Mitchell spun around—it was June Shaw, of course. He turned briefly to the viewer.

'Keep at it. Let me know when you've re-established contact—and that had better be soon!' He angrily switched off the viewer and stared at the scientist. She slid fluidly into his chair and watched him silently. God!—she was something! Expert application of make-up made the bruising he had given her almost invisible. She looked as though she hadn't a care in the world—how did this dangerous, beautiful woman do it?

His eyes narrowed.

'And what the hell do you want?'

She did not reply immediately, and watched a blue-grey cloud of smoke fade as it spiralled upward from her freshly-reddened lips. When she spoke, it was as if she was musing over a recent assignment in the bedroom.

'Neither of us can benefit from this situation. I came along to help you, darling.'

Mitchell conquered his twin desires to either knock her to the floor or pull her into an unbreakable embrace.

'And your plan to stop your bomb ripping this entire galaxy apart?'

Shaw smiled as if he had said something silly but childishly adorable.

'A painfully obvious one, Douglas. You couldn't stop the Controller from launching Pholos, but you can stop it from being launched.'

'And what is that supposed to mean?'

'Pholos was assembled and serviced in space by the use of short-range scouts. You can use one to ferry you over and cut the motor.'

Mitchell put a hand to his forehead. Yes, it was obvious! Why hadn't he realised there was a simpler solution than trying to resurrect the control panel from its mass of fused metals and splintered crystals? Sudden hope flared through him like an electric shock.

'I'd better hurry,' he snapped. 'It's only thirty minutes until departure!'

Shaw patted the bulge of an automatic in her hip pocket.

'You don't know an ion drive from an ironing board. We are going over, darling.'

***

Short-range scouts are two-person short-range craft, completely unstreamlined and with a transparent bubble at their blunt noses through which the occupants can see their surroundings. Mitchell ran across the floor and pressed the control that allowed ingress to the scout.

'You first, Douglas dear,' smiled Shaw, indicating the door with a slight toss of her head. Both snapped the visors of their EVA suits shut, and from then on their voices were only heard to each other, somewhat tinnily, over the short-range radios. Mitchell glanced back at her.

'You know you don't look quite so alluring in that get-up. I could almost fall out of love with you.'

'Make sure you don't,' she hissed, 'Otherwise, you'll learn to love my automatic.'

Mitchell shrugged and climbed in.

'Hurry it up,' she snapped, 'this isn't a training exercise in your pathetic college. You've got twenty minutes!'

The mighty hangar doors slid open, and silently the scout nudged out of the confines of Space Station Triton-1. Out in space, they saw to starboard the immense bulk of Triton, its weird cantaloupe terrain illuminated by the gentle radiance of Neptune-light. But to port was Neptune itself, now in full phase, an immense disc of blue-green splendour. Mitchell saw the great dark storms which marred the peaceful cloud surface; it was impossible to believe those storms were as big as Terrestrial continents. He saw wispy cirrus clouds rising high above the pastel-blue cloud deck, looking achingly like the smaller ones he had looked down upon on leaving Terrestrial orbit, in what now seemed a lifetime ago.

But his attention was directed directly ahead where he knew Pholos would be, now unfortunately at the maximum distance from Triton-1 on its elliptical orbit. Instead of the needle shape he was used to in the viewers, it was just a silvery first-magnitude star.

'Motor,' murmured Mitchell to himself, and instantly he felt himself pressed back into his seat as the scout began to accelerate.

'Fifteen minutes,' Shaw said through gritted teeth. 'Hurry, you fool—we're not going to make it!'

Pholos was many black and empty kilometres from the station, and scouts are not built for speed. Slowly, agonisingly slowly, Pholos grew larger before them, gradually turning first from a bright star to a splendidly brilliant star, and then to a discernible streamlined construction of humanity. However, the scout's radar showed it was still many minutes away. Finally, just as Mitchell began to turn the vessel for a close approach, a pale blue glow appeared at the stern of the probe; a light so pale, so diffuse, so gentle, it was like a calm sea viewed through gauze.

The probe's ion drive had fired.

'Failed,' he groaned, 'so close, so bloody close!'

'Not yet,' Shaw said. Her voice sounded calm, but Mitchell could hear the immense strain beneath her cultured vowels. 'Ion drives take some time to reach their top impulse. We can still rendezvous. You can chase her, can't you?'

'Not normally—the strain on these small engines will be immense.' He groaned. 'But we've got to!'

'And what will happen if the strain is too great?'

Mitchell reached for the boost lever.

'You're the mad scientist. You like explosions, don't you?'

The scout strained until every rivet and seam creaked; the roar of the motors leapt several octaves and both occupants felt a mighty hand push them deep into their seats. Mitchell glanced almost fearfully at the radar screen, but the blip that marked Pholos was moving terrifyingly closer to the edge of the screen—and out of reach.

'Not fast enough. I'll have to burn most of the fuel in one go!'

The rocket nozzles of the small vessel blazed white hot as they erupted blue fury. The control panel disappeared in a red mist as Mitchell's brain was drained of blood under a savage acceleration. His arms felt like lead as he felt, rather than saw, the controls before him. Was that a scream he heard from Shaw?

The motors died, roared back into incandescent life, died again. And then in a scream of high-pitched mechanical screams, they thundered again and kept on thundering.

Shaw pointed at the dial showing the state of the motors. 'Must stop,' she panted, 'it's deep in the red!' She hurled herself at Mitchell. He fought off her frenzied blows and flung her back into her chair. He cut the tortured motors, and a great silence crashed over them like a massive wave.

'It's OK, Ice Maiden. We're matching speeds with Pholos. I guess you have emotions like real women after all.'

She lifted her head and, once again, stilled her fear in a heartbeat.

'Very well done, Douglas. I may have underestimated you. It seems what you lack in theoretical understanding, you make up for with certain practical skills. I won't make that mistake again.' Her attention was caught by something on the radar screen. 'What's that? It's too diffuse to be Pholos.'

Mitchell followed her gaze and frowned.

'You're right. It's not a single object.'

Then he remembered.

'It's the debris cloud from a smash-up of some KBOs a while ago.'

He frowned again: this time more strongly. Were the resultant fragments on an impact trajectory for Pholos? There had been no danger of collision on the probe's original course, but now that it had been reversed—perhaps there was. 'We'd better keep a watch on it. It's certainly going to pass close to us.'

The scout swept on, powered by the momentum of their original mad flight. Mitchell didn't know whether the main motors would ever fire again.

Pholos became visible again in the starry maze and rapidly grew until it filled most of the field of their vision. Mitchell had become so used to seeing the probe as a small toy-like object in the viewers and windows that it was hard to believe this immense object was the actual vessel.

Shaw looked up from another screen where rapidly changing numbers and symbols were displayed.

'The scout will only match Pholos's speed for twenty minutes before falling back. After that the gap will rapidly become too great for us to cross in these suits.'

Mitchell gave a short burst on the lateral jets and turned the scout through a right angle into a closer course alongside the speeding missile. He checked the drift with a burst on another jet and looked up. Pholos was now only thirty metres away, and all they could see was the vast silvery curvature of the hull, blotting out the stars.

'Let's go,' he said, reaching for the tools they would need on Pholos. The two space-suited figures crossed the distance between the two ill-matched vessels on short puffs of compressed gas, landing on its reflective surface a shade too rapidly for his comfort. He glanced at Shaw, even though it was not necessary for him to do that to make himself heard. 'Let's hope you can remember how this thing works. How are you going to disable the drive?'

'I'm not,' came the surprising reply, 'if I do that, the authorities will be able to examine this probe, and our work will be exposed. We will be the ones to decide when we emerge into the daylight. But with the drive functioning at full thrust, the probe will be moving much too fast when it crosses Earth's orbit for any normal ship to board it.'

'Then what are we doing here?'

'Oh, Douglas, it must be terribly difficult trying to live without a brain. We are going to disconnect the bomb, of course. There will be no awfully big bang, and Earth will go on as before, blissfully unaware of our existence, and with only the poor old wreck of a Controller to blame for wasting all that money. We in the League of Lords will have to devise a new strategy, of course, but we are more than capable of that. Now to work—open cover Inspection Cover B-Delta, my little handyman.'

The grotesque shape that contained Dr June Shaw pointed at a rectangular shape protruding slightly from the smooth metal some ten metres away.

Mitchell noticed that in her excitement, she had given away the name of the shadowy organisation she worked for. But did that matter? Would he survive to tell anyone? Thrusting that thought away, he unscrewed the cover and shone his flashlight into the cavity revealed.

'This circular object looks like it doesn't belong here.'

'Correct, my love. That's what we're looking for. Five hundred grams of osmium—everything else is the control mechanism. The thick wire you see connects the neutral matter to the control. The wire sends the instruction to activate the dampening field. It's timed to detonate in the inner Oort Cloud—but any severe impact would set it off. Such as contact with the Sun's atmosphere.

'And then—*Kablooey!*'

She's relaxed. She thinks it's all over, Mitchell thought to himself. *Well, perhaps it is.*

'Anything else I need to know? Do I have to disconnect things in a specific order?'

'Nope. The mechanism is very complex, but there are no booby traps in the connections, because we never thought anyone would be tampering with it once the probe had been launched into deep space. So any disruption to the circuits will render it inoperative, and all our worries will be over. Pholos and five hundred grams of heavy metal will just merge harmlessly into the photosphere. Now, I'd love to spend some time with you explaining how it all works, but I'd like to get back for my evening cocktail, and I'm afraid it's all rather a long way above your pay grade.'

Mitchell was about to reply when he caught a movement at the periphery of his vision. He spun round just in time to see an irregular lump of grey-white material shoot past their heads and disappear sunward. Shaw had seen it too.

'What was that?'

'It's a piece of material from that KBO collision I told you about. The outer fringe of the debris cloud must be passing close to us.'

'Oh, is that all? Now come on, lover—just point your burner at the exact centre of the thing and full power for three minutes.'

Mitchell obeyed. The burner emitted a hungry lance of eye-rending energy, forcing him to avert his gaze several times. The metal glowed red, then yellow, softened and then flowed in viscous drops over the edges of the dread device.

'Three minutes and twenty seconds, that should do it. Your filthy bomb is dead. And now…'

He stood up and turned to face Shaw—and stopped. She was pointing her automatic at his heart.

'Oh, I see,' he said grimly. 'The pay-off, I presume.'

Shaw's helmet nodded. Mitchell wondered if she was smiling inside it or was perhaps just a little bit regretful.

'Oh, my poor dear darling. I'm afraid you are the only one outside our group to know of our existence. You were much too busy with the Controller's nonsense to file any report about naughty little me. We in the League will have to think again and delay our coup to remove those ape-men on Earth from power. But we are patient, and we plan for the long term—that's the mark of intelligence, you see. Believe me, I shall mourn your passing. I really was beginning to like you.'

'If only I could say it was mutual,' he growled. 'But you'd better hurry up, beautiful. The scout is falling behind.' He gestured over Shaw's shoulder. Instinctively she turned to look, and Mitchell brought the burner up, aiming for her helmet. But it took too long to reach full power, and only a comparatively weak flame licked hungrily over her darkened faceplate. A small crack formed, but it showed no sign of spreading or deepening. She was safe.

She took several steps backward.

'My, that was a good one, Douglas! Maybe you do have something hidden in your underpants, after all. This really is too, too bad. I shall weep for seconds after I execute you.'

She lifted the automatic, and, once again, it was aimed for his heart.

This really is it, Mitchell thought grimly, *Earth is safe from the bomb, but how long before this gang of maniacs tries again?*

But suddenly, everything changed. Another fragment from the debris cloud was on an impact trajectory. One moment Shaw was standing there; triumphant; confident; glorying in her achievements—the next a spinning shard sliced into her neck, neatly severing her head from her shoulders. Blood spurted out in a crazy fountain, simultaneously freezing and subliming in the vacuum, and Shaw's body slowly toppled at Mitchell's feet in a zero-g fall.

Mitchell stood astounded at this incredible turn of events. He was instantly aware that fragments were hurtling past him from a radiant almost directly behind Pholos. The probe was almost in the centre of the debris swarm, not at its edge.

He had to get back! He looked for the scout and when he found it, was horrified to see it was now much farther away than when they had crossed over. Pholos was accelerating on its one-way mission to the surface of the sun!

He spun back to the corpse that had once housed one of the most brilliant minds in the Solar system. Somehow, he couldn't leave what remained of her to such a fate—surely, she deserved better than that?

He attached her body to his own suit with the safety wire and with a puff of gas, launched them both off the shining surface of the doomed missile. What if he couldn't reach the scout? The suits had only so much air as they were designed for work near the station where people could easily return to safety.

He switched on his distress beacon. He was not so far from Space Station Triton-1 that they wouldn't pick it up. The station was no longer identifiable, although he knew one of the very bright stars in his vision must be his erstwhile home.

In that dot of light people would be trying to make sense of all that had happened; interviewing the Controller; seeking Dr Shaw's advice. He would see them again!

He fixed the growing image of the scout in his gaze.

And then it happened.

There was one more impact trajectory to be followed to its bitter conclusion.

A spinning chunk of rock and ice struck the scout full-on, and both disintegrated into a million spinning shards.

Mitchell's mind reeled as he saw his hope explode, just as the scout had come so close that he felt he could have reached out and touched it.

Shaw had won! If his rescuers arrived just after his oxygen ran out, no one would ever know of his acts of heroism out here in the cold wastes near Neptune! The League of Lords conspiracy would go on unchecked; unheard of; unsuspected. It would grow in strength and power, and its next blow would be unstoppable. There was no way of getting a message to the authorities at this distance.

Or was there?

Shaw's body was still attached. He rotated it, and, for a moment, they faced each other in an obscene mockery of the sexual act that he had wanted so much. But he pulled slightly away and turned his burner to minimum aperture and maximum power. He knew it did not have much power, and his message would have to cram the most meaning into the fewest symbols. So using the narrow ardent flame, he wrote on her breast plate:

I stop bom on phol shaw resp arrest her staff

The flame flickered and died. He could write no more. Now all he could do was wait.

Grimly, he turned himself so he could look in the direction that his saviours would come from.

And he waited.

NEVER LOOK BACK

They say you should never look back. Well, that's certainly true in my case. I hope I have time to explain why! When time travel was perfected around 2047, the travellers were told that on no occasion were they to visit earlier versions of themselves. Even though the authorities were pretty sure that the universe does not permit temporal paradoxes, it was thought that the danger of psychological damage was too great.

I begged to differ. I thought that I was already psychologically damaged. I couldn't make friends easily and had never had a proper relationship with a woman. I put it all down to my younger self being an introverted bookworm, too busy messing around with fossils, books showing multicoloured portraits of very improbable-looking dinosaurs, and looking through cheap telescopes trying to find alien life instead of getting out and meeting people (i.e. girls). I couldn't remember even kicking a football, let alone kissing a girl.

So that bright sunny day, I took out my time phone and set the controls for the year of my 14th birthday. We call it a phone because it is the same size as the old mobile phones and has lots of numbers on it. You simply key in the year you want to appear in, remembering to remember that there is only enough charge for two hops (i.e. *There* and *Back*).

And so it was that I materialised outside my parents' house on the day I had chosen. It had to be that day because I knew my long-suffering mother and father would be out of the way for several hours. And sure enough—there I was, looking through a magnifying glass at some nondescript toadstool. He saw me arrive, so I didn't have to explain that I was a time traveller. It took a little while longer to convince him that I was him and he was me. It's a little difficult for a 14-year-old to believe that one day he'll be a wrinkled old man.

How do you start telling a boy that he's messing his life up? He stared at his shoes while I got increasingly angry with him.

'What's wrong with being interested in space and fossils and stuff?' he eventually mumbled. I hadn't realised how weak and whiny my voice had been. No wonder the girls didn't like me/him.

'Look!' I finally snapped, barely restraining myself from giving the little wimp a good slap across his pimpled face. 'Let's go inside and have a coffee. I can't stay much longer.'

As we went in, he quizzed me about how to operate the time phone. I must admit he was a quick learner. In the kitchen, I growled, 'Make us two coffees. You can manage that, can't you?'

I remembered where his/my/our bedroom was, so while he/I was fumbling with trying to get the lid off the coffee jar, I allowed a little wave of nostalgia to get the better of me. I decided to take a quick look.

I groaned when I went in—the place was stuffed with plastic models of dinosaurs looking even more improbable than I remembered, and on the wall was a big poster of a Tyrannosaurus Rex chomping on some helpless herbivore. Not a soccer magazine on the bed (nor a girly magazine under the bed either).

What was wrong with this boy? Obsessed with dinosaurs, of all things!

Then I froze—I'd heard the unmistakable sound downstairs of the time phone warming up—I'd left it on the kitchen table!

I rushed back down and tore the glowing phone from his skinny fingers. Too late—he'd already keyed some date in!

There was a kaleidoscopic flash and the indescribable feeling of being hurled through time.

So here I am. From the date on the phone, I calculate that I'm about 100,000 years before the asteroid impact brings an end to the Mesozoic Era. But I don't have to worry about that. I've already seen one carnosaur, and they really do look just as improbable as the pictures, although perhaps not quite so colourful. I think there's a ferocious-looking moving around in those big trees near the swamp.

In fact I

THE BOOK OF LIFE

R aj Patel was a great reader and so was a regular visitor to his local library. He was an omnivorous reader and generally didn't mind what genre of fiction he chose to read, although biographies were his favourite. He found it quite hard to nod off at night if he didn't have a book, so as soon as he finished one, he went back for his next one.

There was nothing unusual about that day. It was an unremarkable Saturday in an unremarkable borough. The library was unremarkable too, although it did have a good stock of non-fiction, which suited Raj. He found a lot of modern fiction quite unpleasant and much preferred the classics like Dickens, Trollope and Hardy. But, as has been said, he really enjoyed a biography, even if it was of someone who had not left much of a ripple on the great pond of life.

On that day, which seemed very ordinary but in fact was anything but, he spent quite some time walking back and forth among the racks of non-fiction, but it was beginning to look like he had read all the biographies the library had to offer. Raj frowned; he didn't like the thought of having to go back home with a western or a book the size of suitcase about dwarves and magic swords, or, quelle horreur, some childish story about spaceships! Just as he was about to turn back to the fiction section his right foot touched something. Looking down, Raj found he had almost stepped on a very old-looking book. On picking it up he discovered that the title was almost completely obscured by a thick layer of grey dust that looked like it had been there for three hundred years. He brushed the grime away and found himself looking at words in very small print which read: "The Book of Life". Was it an old biology textbook? He opened it and was puzzled to find that the pages were white and supple, not at all what one would expect from the cover. The only odd thing about the inside was that the font was a bit old-fashioned, using a clunky Gothic-looking serif font.

He read the first few pages. It was indeed a highly detailed biography, although relating the life of someone he had never heard of: one Carla Andretti. He skimmed rapidly through the first few chapters, looking for some unusual or noteworthy event. Finding none, he turned to the last few happenings in the dear lady's life and was stunned to discover that she had been trampled to death at the foot of the Spanish Steps in Rome by a bull African elephant which had been in the madness of *musth* at the time!

How had this unlikely event happened? Immediately he decided to borrow the book and took it to the counter. The middle-aged librarian stared at the book for several minutes until Raj had begun to think that the gentleman had entered some transcendent mental state. Finally, that worthy looked up and said: 'Strange—I don't think I've ever seen this book before. I don't think it's one of ours.'

Raj shrugged. 'Well, I'd still like to take it out.'

The librarian looked a little worried. 'Hmm, this is most irregular. I can't enter it onto the computer.

But' he added, seeing the mixture of annoyance and disappointment on Raj's face, 'I suppose I could make a written note.'

Having done so, he handed the tome to Raj, who walked quickly home. It was quite a long walk, but as Raj couldn't afford a car, he had no choice but to make the best of things. At least it wasn't raining. On arriving he made himself his usual Saturday lunchtime coffee and sat down to investigate how the unfortunate Carla had found herself face-to-face with a mad elephant in the Eternal City. He decided to skip to the penultimate chapter to see how events had unfolded towards their tragic conclusion. He did so but was astounded to find the pages were blank. But they hadn't been when he had skimmed past them in the library! He worked backwards from that chapter.

Blank.

Blank.

Raj sat back heavily in his armchair. What had happened—had he taken the wrong book to the desk? He looked at the cover. No—it was the same book; it had the title he had read in the aisle: "The Book of Life". He studied the cover closely for the first time. There was something odd about the binding; it felt somehow strange under his fingers. He held it close to his eyes. No, he thought, it can't be! Under close inspection, the covering seemed to have little pores in it as if—as if it were made from skin!

Then a warning voice seemed to rise from his deep subconscious: **"Do not open this book again. Throw it away. Better still, burn it and throw the ashes into a deep, fast flowing river. Do not open this book again!"**

He sat there for quite some time; his mind whirling.

Raj was not a man to be easily spooked. He believed that everything had a logical, mundane, quotidian explanation. There was nothing weird going on here. Obviously he was the victim of a practical joke and the librarian was one of the perpetrators. This was probably something they did from time to time on their established customers. No doubt in a few days Raj and the librarian would be exchanging a few belly-laughs about how funny the whole thing had been. Swapping the real book for one composed entirely of blank pages — hilarious!

Feeling reassured, he opened the book to see if there was a funny message on the first page — and stopped dead.

The first page was not blank.

It read: "Raj took the Book of Life from the library and sat down to read it. He was at first slightly alarmed and then annoyed to find the book appeared to be entirely blank."

He shut the book at once with a loud bang and dropped it on the floor.

This was not right. He was sure the entire book had been blank a few seconds ago. How could there be words on pages when there had been no words before?

No, no, he thought to himself, calm down man! Have you not heard of inks that only appear when warmed? This was obviously how this simple parlour trick had been performed. Still, he conceded, it was well done.

With a half-amused smile, he picked up the book again and turned to the first page again. And frowned.

There were more words.

"Raj spent a quiet Saturday watching television and went to bed early, feeling strangely tired. Sunday was quiet as well, but he was both worried and excited by the approach of work on Monday. He had a feeling that his boss was going to say something important to him. And, of course, there was Caitlin."

He dropped the book again. Now it was telling him what was going to happen! And how did the librarian know about Caitlin!

He put the book away and vowed never to open it again.

He sent out for a takeaway and watched television in the evening.

Finally, a growing headache forced him to abandon his desultory viewing and caused him to decide that he might as well go to bed.

It was only after he had been in bed for ten minutes that he realised that he had gone to bed early.

The following day he woke with the memory of a crazy dream about a mysterious old book that seemed to…

He sat up straight in bed. It hadn't been a dream.

He ate his breakfast slowly and deliberately, throwing the occasional glance at the book which lay closed on the sofa. Should he open it or just throw it away? He walked over, coffee mug in hand, and stared down at it. Then with a look of determination, he picked it up and placed it in the waste paper basket. No more meddling with things he didn't understand!

The rest of the day passed quietly. Several times he walked over to the waste paper basket and stared down at the book. On one occasion, his hand actually reached out and almost touched the book as if it had some eldritch power of compulsion: that it actually wanted to be picked up and opened! But he had fought off the compulsion and instead had gone out for a walk around the nearby park to get himself pleasantly tired.

Finally, after some more of watching TV programmes that he was only half-interested in he went to bed at the normal time.

He had NOT read the book!

***

It was a grey, rainy morning on Monday; the kind that depresses the soul and brings visions of Caribbean beaches to the mind of the hapless commuter, complete with strawberry daiquiris and strawberry blondes, the latter seductively lounging on an extremely welcoming lounger.

Raj stared at the window; *at* it not *through* it because the wriggling rain-worms on the outer surface had turned the external world into a messy multicoloured blur, looking much as if an untalented child had been given unlimited access to a range of paint pots and wet paper.

What kind of a day was he going to have at work?

He soon found out.

Caitlin ignored his morning greeting in the same Siberian manner as she normally did, not even looking up from the photocopier over which she had somehow managed to drape herself, displaying such an amazing amount of tanned thigh that it seemed impossible that any of the male employees would be able to get any work done.

Raj gave a sickly smile as he passed, manfully resisting the temptation to look back at the photocopier and its near-occupant, trying to pretend to those out of earshot that Caitlin had actually acknowledged him.

Reluctantly occupying his cubicle, he turned on his computer and scanned the obligatory company news bulletin that flashed up. The scanning of the bulletin was obligatory because his boss had a nasty habit of asking penetrating questions that only eager employees who had actually read the tedious thing could possibly answer.

Hmm. There was a vacancy in the Stuttgart office. Well, some young office toady who fawned on the boss's every word would surely get that. There was no point in studying it—the boss had the power to fill those vacancies and it was absolutely certain that he would give it to some sycophantic yes-man. You could tell who they were because for some reason they all had distinctly brown noses.

The day wore on. The boss made one of his rare perambulations around the office, stopping at the desks of his favourites. Raj noted with extreme irritation that he seemed to be spending an inordinate amount of time in Caitlin's cubicle. How long does it take to check a pile of photocopies?

Finally, he passed Raj's desk. Raj gave him what he hoped was a "Hiya buddy" grin which succeeded only in making the boss look slightly startled, as if he had been approached by a total stranger in a secluded alley. And that was that. The highlight of Raj's day.

The day ground on, plumbing new depths of Kafkaesque futility. Raj managed to exchange glances with Caitlin, but he might just as well have been staring at a codfish on a slab, so glassy was the returning gaze.

It was still raining on the way back, and due to the fading light, there was even less to see through the bus window. Plus, Raj was unable to claim a seat as a group of giggling young women were occupying his usual seating area.

Back home, Raj defrosted a microwaveable TV Dinner and contemplated the meaning of existence. A meaning which seemed extremely difficult to discover at present.

As his stomach began its epic struggle to digest the TV Dinner, he found his thoughts returning to the book.

What did he have to lose? At least it brought a new thrill into his days; a frisson of excitement of dealing with something different, something a little on the weird side, something—dare he say it— mysterious?

His mind at last made up, he crossed to the waste paper basket and retrieved the book. Turning to the page that referenced the current day Raj read: "It was a dull day at the office. Nothing noteworthy occurred. Neither the boss nor Caitlin took any notice of him. Raj wondered if anything he was doing in his cubicle was of any value. Did anybody even read his reports?

"On returning home, Raj decided to open the book again. Once again, he had had the thought that the boss was about to say something important to him. And he had noticed a mischievous twinkle in Caitlin's eyes. Time would tell!"

Raj sat back with the book open in his lap. Had there been a mischievous twinkle in her eyes? Yes, perhaps there had been! And the way the boss had suddenly stopped when Raj had grinned at him—maybe he had been about to say The Important Thing!

Raj turned to where the Tuesday chapter should be—but it was blank, of course. On the rest of the Monday section it merely said: "Raj spent the rest of the evening in a state of barely suppressed excitement. Unfortunately, this was interrupted by a bad case of indigestion which meant that he could not enjoy his normal TV programmes. As result, he was forced to go to bed early."

Raj put the book down and went to his medicine cabinet to find his antacid tablets.

***

Tuesday dawned dim and unpromising, with the entire sky seemingly shut off by a single dismal grey cloud through which the sun had tried, valiantly but unsuccessfully, to send a lonely sunbeam to the crowded streets below.

The bus journey was as soul-sapping as usual, and Raj had scant hopes for any uplifting experiences as he finally made it to his office. Caitlin was leaning over the photocopier again—did that girl have anything else on her job description? He decided to ignore her but—wait! Was that a mischievous twinkle in her eyes? As it had been quite a while since Raj had last seen a mischievous twinkle it took it some time to reach the momentous conclusion that it was indeed such a twinkle. By which time, something even more mind-blowing had occurred. Caitlin had said: 'Morning, Raj.'

Raj was so stunned that for some seconds his vocal apparatus refused to do anything at all than to make noises reminiscent of a marsh frog about to depart for the Great Hereafter. But finally, he managed to say, 'Morning Caitlin'; although the utterance was still somewhat on the strangulated side.

In his cubicle, he felt so disconcerted that he actually started to read the company news as it rolled up the screen. While half his mind was occupied with Caitlin the other half somehow took in the information that an announcement of the Stuttgart appointment was imminent. He could not suppress a grunt of disapproval on reading that and wondered which of the boss's many blue-eyed favourites would be the lucky man.

The morning wore on. Although his mind kept flashing back to the delicious cleavage he had caught a glimpse of earlier, he still managed to complete his report on the sales projection for the next two quarters. No sooner had he pressed the "Send" button than he became aware of someone standing directly behind him. Slowly he turned, and his heart missed quite a few beats when he discovered that it was the boss standing over him.

'Good work, Raj' was the unexpected message the boss delivered to Raj's disbelieving ears, 'I was reading over your shoulder—I hope you don't mind. Your use of multivariate analysis was very apt. And your regression calculations—spot on.'

Raj's puzzlement increased. The techniques the boss was mentioning were a standard, built-in module of the software on his computer. All Raj had needed to do was click on a green icon marked "Perform Analyses" and the results popped up automatically. Was the boss drunk?—a howler monkey fresh from the Amazonian rainforest could have done exactly the same thing; maybe quicker. But no—there was no smell of whisky emanating from his superior. This was Tuesday, after all; not Friday afternoon.

The boss then did something which Raj had never seen before—he smiled. It was an odd smile as if that worthy was doing something that his lips were unaccustomed to; at least in Raj's presence.

'Join me in my office, please Raj,' the boss said. Raj's heart missed a few more beats. The last time he had been in that dread domain was to receive a ticking-off for poor timekeeping. What had he done now? Had the boss been sadistically ladling out false praise while preparing to send Raj packing to some inferior position in the company or, even worse, give him three weeks' notice? A vision of his most recent bank statement danced leeringly before Raj's eyes as he followed his boss's broad back into the inner sanctum. Neither looked very reassuring.

'Sit down, my boy,' the boss said cheerfully; Raj made no demur even though he suspected that he was actually several years the older. 'I expect you're wondering why I called you in.'

'Yes, Mr Atkins.'

'Well, it's about your work.'

Oh no! This was it! The earlier comment had been cruel sarcasm, after all. What would be his punishment?

'Well, I want to tell you that I am extremely pleased with both the quality and the quantity of what you produce. You have good old-fashioned values, my boy. Lots of the young men in this place think that the world owes them a living. They've had people tell them how wonderful and special they are, all their lives. I dare say that's never happened to you. As a result, they think that all they have to do is turn up, and I'll shower them with money that they can spend on drugs and booze. And the girls are just as bad—they're either leaning over the men in low-cut dresses or painting their nails. While you—you just get on with it, day after day. Never complaining, never asking for a raise or some special favour. Just good old-fashioned hard work.'

Raj felt a strange giddiness creep through his body, starting with the back of his head and slowly working its way forward. Was this all part of some evil scheme to humiliate him? Was it some senior management joke that had gone too far? Was it too late to join the union and ask their advice? The boss's next words were like the Fairy Godmother declaiming: 'You shall go to the ball!'

'That's why I'd like to offer you the Stuttgart job.'

Raj just sat upright in the chair; his eyes seemed fixed on some wondrous sight located at infinity.

'It'll be on a temporary basis to start with,' the boss continued, apparently not noticing that his employee had entered a trance-like state, 'while you prove yourself. But I have no doubt you'll cut the mustard.'

Eventually, the silence grew too much for him, and he said, slightly irritated by the lack of exhilaration on the part of his chosen appointee, 'What do you say?'

Raj snapped out of it. If this was a dream, then he had no intention of waking up. He had seen the salary on offer for the Stuttgart post and, for someone like him, it was little short of life-changing.

'Well Mr Atkins, all I can say is that I'm deeply honoured. This is more than I'd dared hoped for. But I can tell you this—I won't let you down. I won't disappoint you or this wonderful company.'

The boss smiled again; and this time it seemed completely natural and unforced.

'I hoped you'd say that, my boy. Personnel will be in touch with you over the next day or so to finalise the arrangements. I expect you to move to Stuttgart in about a fortnight. We'll take care of the administrative odds and sods—no need for you to worry about them.

'Well, congratulations!'

With that, Raj found himself looking down at the boss's outstretched hand. He shook it warmly, trying to ignore the rather unpleasant moistness and softness of the other's hand and still in a daze, walked back to his cubicle without really noticing anything at all on the way. He tried to carry on with his work as normal, but it was hard to get involved; after all what had he to prove?

As the day wore on, he became conscious that more and more glances were being directed at him, some of which became transmuted into overtly hostile stares. He grinned. The office grapevine was still operating it seemed! Soon the whole company would know how one apparently insignificant little mouse-clicker had scooped the prize! He suddenly remembered the book—what had it said—"the boss was about to say something important to him"? You could say that again!

Finally, the hour reached the earliest time he could finish work and that's exactly what he did. Ferguson tried to impede his exit by moving in front of him. Ferguson—the one he had always suspected would be the one to get the plum in the pudding. Ferguson had obviously felt the same way because his tone was one of overt hostility.

'Cat got your tongue, Raj? Is there something you want to tell us, we ordinary wage slaves?'

'Oh, not much,' Raj replied airily, 'Just got the Stuttgart job, that's all!'

Ferguson looked crestfallen; he had obviously been hoping that the rumour was false.

'You little shit,' he finally hissed from between clenched teeth, 'what the fuck have you got that I haven't?'

Raj intended just to shrug his shoulders and move on but, as he began to do so, he suddenly stopped and, looking the bemused Ferguson full in the face, he said mysteriously: 'I've got the book!'

On returning home, Raj was so excited that he didn't feel like defrosting another TV Dinner, so he treated himself to Home Delivery pizza. As he was munching triumphantly through his treat, he suddenly thought to check his experiences against the book. Turning to the Tuesday section, he was not in the least surprised to find that additional text had appeared.

Smiling to himself and being very careful not to dribble mozzarella on the pages, he read: "After the boss had given him the good news, Raj left work early and, on arriving home, decided to order a celebratory pizza. The increase in his take-home pay would be truly life-changing! However, when he was a little over halfway through the pizza an unpleasant thought struck him: If he was moving to Stuttgart, how was he ever to get it on with Caitlin?"

Raj stopped munching as if struck by a thunderbolt. Good God, yes! Why hadn't he thought of that earlier? What to do, what to do?

He glanced down at his meal: he was a little over halfway through consuming it.

And there was something else—did the book look a little thinner, as if it no longer held as many pages as yesterday?

***

Raj spent a troubled night. Money isn't everything, a little voice kept telling him; there are such things as relationships, such things as love and—let's face it—such things as SEX.

When the normal getting-up time finally arrived, he seriously considered going in to work and telling the boss that he had changed his mind and was quite happy to stay in London as a poor but honest, minor cog in a great big machine and that he could best serve the wonderful company that he was privileged to work in by staying firmly put.

Having swallowed the last cornflake, he wondered—could the book help him? Had it updated itself to Wednesday's events yet? Even if it meant missing his usual bus, he'd see if its wisdom could help him find a way out of this great dilemma. He opened it at the Wednesday page and was gratified to see a large mass of print was already there. Eagerly he scanned the sentences.

"Raj had come to realise that as a man going places, in fact, an international executive, he would be much more interesting to women than hitherto. No doubt Caitlin would be one of the many females who would be trying to catch his eye."

Thunderstruck, he leaned back in his chair. Of course, it was bound to be the case! What would he do without this book? He was so dumb that he really didn't deserve all the help it was giving him. What had he done to be so lucky?

With a knowing smile on his face, he virtually leapt onto the bus, quite alarming the little old lady who had only just got on before him.

Caitlin was there as he arrived, draped over the photocopier as usual. But this time as soon as she saw him, she stood up, smoothing her tight dress over her thighs, and turned to block his way further into the office.

'Hi, Raj!' she said, almost as if she had stationed herself there just so she would be the first to speak to him, 'My, aren't you the go-getter. Congratulations, you lucky devil. Why, I almost feel like giving you a great big kiss!'

'And what's stopping you?' Raj enquired, amazed at his own audacity.

Caitlin looked a little surprised; this didn't seem like the Mr Meek-and-Mild she'd been used to but, having gone so far, there was no harm in going a little further. She placed her hands on Raj's shoulders in one fluid movement—being almost exactly as tall as he was—and gave him a quick peck on the lips. Raj went rigid in more ways than one— that quick pressure of lip on lip, the warmth and moisture of flesh touching flesh—it was heaven! Had there been the slightest feeling of a tongue behind those ambrosial lips? By the time he had decided that only a repeat of the experiment would prove it one way or the other he discovered that Caitlin had picked up her photocopying and taken it to wherever she took the photocopying to—no one seemed quite sure where that was.

Raj decided that he would have to make his move on Caitlin sooner rather than later; that particular kettle seemed to be boiling and he didn't want the heat to go down.

The day ground on—Raj wasn't quite sure whether he was doing any work or not; he remembered pushing some buttons and clicking on some icons on his computer, but he couldn't recall exactly what he'd been doing at the time. There was only one thing on his mind—how to get more of Caitlin. The book had said that Caitlin would now be interested in him—and when had the book been wrong? Why wait any longer?

Putting his computer to sleep, he left the cubicle and strode down the corridor to where he knew Caitlin worked. His stride got a little slower and more hesitant as he approached that hallowed area, but his memory of the assurance given by the book drove him on. Finally, he was there and there was the lovely girl, unfortunately surrounded by a coterie of girls almost as lovely.

Keeping the book firmly in mind, he approached the group of females. As one, they turned and looked at him, making Raj feel somewhat like an absent-minded grouse on the morning of the Glorious Twelfth.

'Oh, hi Caitlin,' he finally managed to say despite having a mouth as dry as the Atacama desert. 'Fancy seeing you here.'

'This is where I work.'

'Oh, is it?'

'Yes. I've worked here for the past four years.'

'Is that right? Well, I never knew that.'

Raj felt that his moment was slipping away. The looks of amusement of the faces of the other girls were getting stronger.

"Done much photocopying today?'

'About the same as usual.'

'Oh. That's good. Don't want you working too hard—ha-ha!'

A silence fell. Raj felt that if he didn't say something meaningful soon the silence would last forever, and his one and only chance would be flushed down the toilet of life.

The book! The book! He chanted mantra-like to himself. It would not fail him!

'Would you like to go out tonight?' he heard someone say. Someone—that was him—*he'd actually said it!*

Caitlin's companions looked at each other. *Had he actually said that?*

Caitlin herself said nothing for what seemed a geological age. Then: 'I'm sorry, Raj. I can't make it tonight.'

Raj's mind spun. The book—it had finally failed him! This was all a terrible mistake! He had misinterpreted that kiss! There had been no tongue! He had humiliated himself in front of all these lovely ladies! He nodded and turned to go.

'But I'm alright for tomorrow night,' Caitlin continued.

The girls all looked at each other at the same time.

Caitlin looked at Raj.

Raj looked at Caitlin.

'It's a date,' he said.

***

The following day Raj spent some time with the boss. Initially his superior had offered a 10% pay rise to go with the promotion, but Raj had held out for 15%. Eventually the boss gave in.

'You're one tough cookie, Raj,' he had said while shaking the hand of his soon-to-be-promoted underling, 'You're going to give them hell when you get to Stuttgart. Maybe I should warn them about what's coming!'

Raj just gave a "You're Damned Right!" *mano a mano* grin in response and sauntered back to his cubicle. There he had something of an unpleasant surprise as Kozynski was waiting for him there.

Kozynski did not look happy.

'What's this I hear about you asking Caitlin out?' he demanded, sitting menacingly on Raj's desk, so close that their legs touched briefly. 'Don't you know she's my girl?'

Raj yawned while putting his arms behind his head.

'I didn't, and neither does she apparently,' he drawled, fixing Kozynski with a gimlet stare. 'She didn't think twice about agreeing to see me. Look like you've been kidding yourself, old chum.'

Kozynski stared in wonderment, as if a worm underfoot had not only turned but whipped out a submachine gun.

'Who the thundering fuck do you think you are?' he spluttered. 'I've heard about the Stuttgart job. They must be smoking some heavy shit to think of giving you that job. The office cleaner would be a better choice!'

Raj smiled. He had the book. He knew everything would be alright. Somehow, he was in complete control of the situation and knew exactly what to do next.

'Yeah, the Stuttgart job. You know I'm looking for a guy to go with me. Help me out; take some of the heat off of me. Sort of Man Friday role. Fair bit of money in it too. I think you might fill the bill, old chum. Interested?'

Kozynski's expression changed in a heartbeat from Vlad the Impaler to Saint Francis of Assisi.

'Stuttgart? Fair bit of money? Interested — are you kidding?'

'I'll see what I can do, old chum.' Raj stood up. 'Shake on it, buddy. But what about Caitlin?'

Kozynski grinned a grin that had a fair percentage of leer in it. 'Caitlin? Shag her brains out, boss—what's it got to do with me?'

Raj left early again, after all, he had a lot to do, not least to check the book to see how the evening would go!

He pulled the Book of Life from amongst the few other volumes he had on his bookshelf. He frowned; it seemed lighter, thinner—how was that possible? He shrugged; after all, he hadn't been weighing the damn thing; he couldn't possibly be sure. With hands that were ever so slightly trembling he turned to section for the evening with lay before him; an evening brimming with untold possibilities.

Gradually his tense face relaxed until at the end of the section, he was positively beaming. This is what he read: "The evening began uncertainly.

Caitlin seemed distant at first as if she wasn't sure she had done the right thing. They talked about work for a while, but the conversation was a little hesitant as Raj had no idea what Caitlin actually did, even after she had told him. After the meal, Caitlin began to mention going home. Raj made his move, but she pushed him away, saying 'No, Raj. This isn't what I want. I like you but I can only ever be a friend to you." But Raj noticed little signs that showed that she was being economical with the truth and persisted. Eventually, she melted into his arms, whispering, "Oh Raj, you've no idea how long I've waited for you to hold me like this!"

'After a period of passionate kissing Raj led her upstairs and ...'

Oh well, you get the idea.

Given the importance of the evening, Raj decided to pull out all the stops. Even though success was preordained, he didn't want it handed to him on a plate; he wanted to do something to earn it! So instead of his usual meal he sent out for a Chinese. And he had some cans of lager on hand if they were needed.

Eventually, there was a knock at the door, and he let his inamorata into his little place. He slipped her coat off and was thrilled to see that she was not exactly overdressed underneath, the blouse especially seemed delightfully flimsy.

Over his Chow Mein, he tried to engage the girl in light conversation, but she seemed somewhat distracted, as if waiting for something to happen. And what did she actually DO in the office? She had told him twice, and he still couldn't get his head around it. Where did all that photocopying fit into things? Where did she take it?

But after what seemed an eternity, she looked up from the last remaining noodle on her plate, smiled sweetly, and said, 'Well, Raj I've had a lovely time. Thank you for this meal. The noodles were delicious, but I really must be going.'

'You haven't finished your lager,' Raj observed.

'Oh, I've had quite enough. Raj, If I didn't know you better, I'd say you were trying to get me drunk!' She stood up.

Raj pushed his chair back, crossed to her, and held one of her hands in two of his.

'Caitlin, I don't think you really want to go home.' And he made as if to kiss her.

She pulled her hand free and placed her palms on his chest as if to push him away.

'Raj, I really like you, but you should know that all I want is for us to be friends. I already have a boyfriend.'

HAD a boyfriend, Raj thought grimly. and found himself unable to suppress a little smile of victory. 'Well, a little kiss goodnight then?'

Again the sweet smile. 'Well, of course. We're friends, aren't we?'

Their lips met. And clung. And eventually, Raj was certain—that was a tongue! The kisses went on, gradually increasing in intensity and energy. Raj felt hard nipples through the thin fabric of her top. And then:

'Oh, Raj, you've no idea how long I've waited for you to hold me like this!'

And the rest of the evening was spent exactly as the Book of Life had specified. Not one single detail was incorrect.

***

Raj spent the next day in a daze. Everything he had ever wanted had come to pass. The office, which had been purgatory, was now paradise. All the men were trying to curry favour with him; the boss didn't seem to mind when he saw Raj playing a game on his computer (which was now most of the time); the other girls were dropping big hints that if he ever got tired of Caitlin, then they were more than ready to step up to the plate. There was a name for this situation, wasn't there? Hadn't some pop star talked about "The Paradise Syndrome" where all one's desires are satisfied, and there's nothing left to want? Well, Raj was pretty sure that he had a few desires which hadn't yet been satisfied; after all, he hadn't gone onto his new salary yet.

And Caitlin was all right, but why settle for one fish when there's a whole ocean of them out there, begging to be reeled in?

He left early yet again, and once home, he spent some time tidying up his bedroom. Good God, how did THAT get on the ceiling?

Eventually getting bored with the gargantuan job of clearing up the mess left after last night's frolics, he idly thought he'd take a quick look at the book. Tomorrow was Saturday, and he wasn't seeing Caitlin till Sunday as she said she was still a bit sore, so he wasn't expecting anything wonderful to be foretold.

Two lines appeared between his eyebrows as he turned to the Saturday section—it was blank. Not a single word, comma or semicolon.

How could NOTHING be happening (or not happening) for one whole day?

It had never happened (or not happened) before. Perhaps the book had decided he needed a rest from all this endless excitement, all this torrent of satisfaction and gratification, all this cornucopia of wonders. Perhaps the human nervous system could be damaged by an overload of ecstasy.

Perhaps.

But it was slightly worrying—a whole day of nothing. He wasn't used to it.

He spent the evening trying to get interested in the usual TV shows, but his mind kept returning to the book, and its unheard-of silence.

The night was spent in a sleep that was fitful. He had an inchoate feeling that something was wrong. It was almost like the first day when he had opened the book and been troubled by formless fears.

The morning came. Still the page was blank.

Ten o'clock—nothing.

Eleven o'clock—nothing.

At midday, he opened the book again, and felt a wave of relief break over him. There were words on the page—his wonders had not ceased!

And then he actually read the words.

"At 12:55 Raj Patel was killed by a heart attack."

WHAT! That was ridiculous—he was 29 and had never felt a twinge! He could leap up the stairs two at a time! There was no heart disease in his family! There…

He stopped. This was the Book of Life. It had never been wrong before. What could he do! How could he stave off doom!

One thing was certain—he had to get to a hospital before 12:55!

He phoned one taxi company. The phone rang and rang, but no one answered. The second answered, but could not get there until 2PM.
Finally, the third said that they would be there at once.

Raj ran out onto the pavement, not bothering to shut the door behind him. He anxiously scanned the busy traffic moving slowly past his house, but after only a few minutes he saw the welcome logo of his taxi coming towards him. Jumping in, he yelled the name of the nearest hospital and the driver, hearing the urgency in Raj's voice, decided that he was a genuine emergency case and sent the taxi hurtling into action.

'Take the canal road!' Raj yelled. He could feel his heart thundering in his chest—could the driver not hear it? The damn organ must be building up to its final paroxysm! Every second counted. 'Faster, man!' he yelled.

The taxi screeched onto the canal road, nearly colliding with a vehicle ambling along in the other direction.

And then, as the Book of Life had foretold, it happened.

There was absolutely nothing wrong with Raj's heart, of course. It was strong enough for another sixty years of pumping.

The taxi driver's heart was a different matter. Already weakened by minor traumas some months earlier, it was put under tremendous strain by the urgency of the situation.

It convulsed into a myocardial infarction.

The driver lost consciousness, the vehicle crashed through the barrier and nosedived into the canal.

The taxi driver was thrown clear and survived. Raj was not and did not.

***

Two months later, Gretchen Mabovitch was perusing the bookshelves in the public library, Lethbridge, Alberta. As part of her Doctoral Thesis "Ordinary People: Their Role in Human History", she was looking for a biography of someone who was not particularly well-known or respected. However, all the volumes she had perused were either of famous people, or people who sincerely thought they were famous.

She was about to give it up and go and get a coffee, when her foot hit something. Bending down, she saw a large, dust-covered book. She picked it up, noticing that the material of the cover felt odd beneath her fingers. The title was partly covered in a thick layer of solidified grime, which, when removed, displayed the title "The Book of Life." Intrigued, she looked inside and was gratified to discover it was a chronicle of a particularly undistinguished young man who had lived in a particularly undistinguished suburb of London, England. Its pages of unrelieved tedium and mind-numbing minutiae seemed just what she had been looking for. Tucking it under an arm, she abandoned her quest and headed straight for the booking-out desk.

The lady sitting there looked mildly surprised when a dusty, ancient-looking book with a strange binding was placed in front of her. There was something about it that repelled her as much as if a long-dead bullfrog had been dropped into the middle of her evening meal.

Looking up at Gretchen, she said: 'Strange—I don't think I've seen this book before. I don't think it's one of ours.'

JUPITER THE KING

Julia Webster shivered as she looked through the crystal window at the howling black hell of Jupiter. It was as if she could feel the weight of thousands of kilometres of roaring, turbulent atmosphere pressing down on the shining, fragile-looking domes of the Valveren.

As she looked out over the oily waves of liquid hydrogen stretching forever out to the indeterminate horizon, she felt depressed and helpless, thinking of how those waves merged into others and then others, on and on into the monstrous global ocean that formed Jupiter's ever-shifting surface. Suddenly the scene was lit by a flash of lightning, a tremendous twisted kris of power: savage, blue-white, caustic. The Valveren domes caught the light of a bolt that could have incinerated a city in an instant and threw its blinding fury into the mist-wreathed darkness, illuminating the swollen crimson udders of an unbroken cloud deck and briefly, it seemed, the impossibly distant line of the horizon.

Simultaneously with the flash, Julia's hands had leapt to her eyes, but still she felt the actinic blast penetrate to her retinas as if her flesh had become transparent under the hammer blow of its violence. Why did she feel that way? She had always known that Valveren engineering could protect her from anything even the King of Planets could deliver. She was in no danger; this region of the planet's pseudosurface was relatively calm, distant as it was from the cyclonic hell of the Great Red Spot.

She turned from the window, feeling strangely tired. There had been a time when the lightning had exhilarated her, when she had felt the joy of being part of this great project, even if her contribution, like that of all the other people here, was inevitably minor. But she had been proud to have been chosen, even if she was like a student collaborating on some grand research project whose ultimate goal was somewhat beyond her.

She shook her head and tried to focus her thoughts. What was this depression? Where was it coming from?

Julia looked around her room and was happy with what she saw: the pastel-coloured televiewer screen, the elegant, minimalist furniture, the soft golden carpeting and the little fountain which formed a bell of seemingly motionless water in the centre of the room. (Valveren science, of course, blocked most of the crushing Jovian gravitational pull, stepping it down to the standard 1g.) On the other side, by a nest of tables, she noticed, as if for the first time, a small wall mirror and felt somehow drawn to it. That mirror must always have been there: why had she not looked into it before? A face which was both familiar and strange met her gaze from within the glass. Her hand went to her eyes: there was a fan of lines radiating from the corner of each one. How long had they been there? The hand moved slowly down the face; yes, there were fine vertical lines reaching down into the lips. She was disturbed by them. They looked unnatural and ugly, yet she had been unaware of them before this instant. Her skin seemed loose and wrinkled in some areas, but in others appeared to barely cover the bone.

Suddenly Julia felt even wearier and, at the same time, frightened by the stranger in the mirror. She turned and slumped into a chair. She turned the window opaque with a quick stab at the remote control and instantly the black, alien ocean was replaced with a soft, pastel radiance. She closed her eyes. For a moment she could almost forget that she was adrift on that monstrous expanse, more overwhelmed in scale than an ant thrown into the Pacific. Only the transcendent science of the Valveren was saving her from being crushed, choked and roasted simultaneously.

Why was she no longer content? Why was there this sudden fear of Jupiter soaking into her brain, where before there had been only pride and excitement? Why…? Her dangling fingers suddenly felt coarse hairs rubbing against them, and beneath the hair, a small, hard-muscled body. Julia smiled.

'Micky,' she chuckled, 'What are you up to?'

She sat up, the tiredness and anxiety washing from her face.

'Come on, you little devil!'

The small Vervet monkey made a scolding noise but jumped onto her lap and lay quiet as Julia ran her fingers through his pelt. She smiled as she smoothed the fur, unaware that the smile forced her nascent facial lines into sharper relief.

Micky, she thought to herself, *What a lousy name for a monkey!*

She had never been very good at choosing names. Just as well, she had never had children; she would probably have named them Jack and Jill, irrespective of their actual genders.

'Still,' she said out loud, 'Micky doesn't seem to mind—do you, Micky?'

The animal looked back at Julia and, not for the first time, she felt the narrowness of the gap between monkey and person as those almost human eyes met her own. Sometimes she felt that there was a mind nearly equal to her own behind those brown orbs, striving to reach out across chasms of silence to make contact. Is this how the Valveren felt on those rare occasions when they attempted communication with people?

She stopped smiling and roughly hugged the monkey to her chest as if embracing a lover. For a moment, she pressed the animal tightly and then, feeling suddenly foolish, held the creature at arms-length and forced another smile.

'Go on, you little devil, get yourself some fruit!' She propelled him toward the fruit bowl, and after a moment's hesitation he loped off into the corner with a banana.

She watched him go and said out loud: 'Come on, Julia, snap out of it. Let's get some work done instead of feeling sorry for yourself!'

Yet the very word "work" stopped her again. What use could human beings be to the Valveren in their grand designs; what use could our own scientists have ever had for creatures like chimpanzees except as experimental animals. Yet that idea, at least, was ridiculous—wasn't it? Carlo would have laughed out loud. Indeed, had laughed out loud on one occasion at the idea that humankind had anything to fear from intelligences other than Terrestrial. For a moment, her room seemed to blur and dissolve; for a moment, she saw again their beach house near San Diego—the sand white under the moonlight—and heard the deep-throated crash of the breakers flinging their powerful spume across the ribbed sand toward them.

For most of that evening, he had displayed that megawatt smile, the smile which had always managed to lift her spirits. Even in the early evening gloom, she could have seen that white, white smile. But there was no difficulty seeing anything given the flood of coloured light that streamed from their windows and open door of their home. The sound of men and women, who had had just a little too much to drink and smoke, rang out from their house, with the occasional belly laugh or giggle cutting through the general chatter. Outside the house, a few groups of people had gathered into little knots; some to caress and fondle, others to dispute and argue. Carlo had been good at both activities, but now he had chosen to argue.

'No, no,' he said, pausing only to take another sip at his long, cold drink, 'that kind of thinking is so old and worn-out, so "Twentieth Century".'

His opponent was as thin and dry as a piece of driftwood that had been lying on the nearby beach for an eternity. He did not have a drink, or for that matter, a smile. He was looking directly at Carlo, as he had all evening, mostly ignoring Julia, even when she had leaned across him, trying to provoke.

'No, Mister Andretti, it is not that simple, as I suspect you know. You believe, do you, that moral advancement must go with scientific advancement?

Everyone knows that the Nazis and Khmer Rouge used flint axes and bone knives whilst writing love songs!'

Carlo's high-voltage smile had not wavered. He was confident in his views.

'No, no, you mustn't set up simple straw men like that, accusing me of some kind of linear extrapolation. Naturally, there must be fluctuations and backward steps. The fact remains that over the decades, there has been a steady turning away from might makes right, a growing contempt for violence.'

The dry man had shaken his head like a tutor dealing with a slow pupil.

'My dear Andretti, you, as a neurophysiologist, should be ashamed to sit there in a drunken stupor spouting such infantile nonsense. Why, I almost prefer to listen to your other little lectures on Chaucer and Spencer, and the other forgotten nobodies you drag up from your hobbies. At least then, you can be excused for not knowing what you're talking about. Does not your own research indicate that morality is simply the expression of a certain pattern of neurons firing, one chosen by natural selection out of an infinity of possible patterns, all equally valid if they aid survival? Why should you think that a truly alien neural network would react in a way that we would recognise or, more to the point, applaud?'

Carlo's smile had at last wavered at this point, and the debate turned a trifle acerbic. The dry man seemed impervious to Carlo's arguments and seemed to be able to draw on Carlo's own esoteric research to support his contentions. Julia had got steadily more bored. This wasn't the kind of party she'd been expecting. She felt far too sober for this late in the evening. Where was the mild flirtation with which she'd planned to employ to arouse a little jealousy in Carlo, leading to a passionate bout of forgiveness in their warm bed? Then, miraculously the debate was over. The dry man must have been satisfied that he had won the argument, for hc finally recognised Julia's existence and gave her a kind of smile, revealing yellowish and surprisingly irregular teeth.

'Well, I wish you luck with your eminent lover, Ms Webster. I do hope for all our sakes, that he never has a practical demonstration of the facetiousness of his beliefs. And with that I must leave you. I think I spy my delectable young friends waving at me to join them amongst the dunes.'

Carlo had leaned forward to deliver one final comment, but Julia had entwined her fingers in his springy black hair and, perhaps a little too roughly, had pulled his head back.

'No—enough is enough, my darling!'

And they had gone back together into the bright warmth of their house, back to the laughter and the levity, back to a world that would soon be gone forever.

It was the following week that the Valveren fleet appeared, gleaming in all the skies of Earth simultaneously and unheralded. No probe or telescope had seen them approach. One instant, they did not exist: the next, they were there; massive, brilliant, intimidating, and so obviously superior to any work of humanity. With little delay, the entities within had mastered the main world languages and quickly reassured the apprehensive billions that there was nothing to fear. Soon humanity learned that the visitors comprised a scouting party which had been exploring worlds deep within the dark vastness that is Laniakea. Their mission had not been to this galaxy at all, but some error in the flux of forces that drove their shimmering craft had flung them out of their planned trajectory and forced them to take refuge in the Milky Way galaxy; in which star system they were now marooned, being unable to calculate the route back to their home world. They had no evil designs on humanity's home planet; indeed, if any world in the Solar system was even remotely suitable for them to inhabit, that world was giant Jupiter, for the Valveren were very different creatures to people. Not fully organic, not fully cybernetic, they were some hypercomplex quantum-level fusion of both states that was difficult for humans to understand. However, now that chance had brought them together, there was much the two races could do to work together for their mutual benefit…

Julia's eyes started open. Had she been asleep? The vision of the past had been so vivid, so tangible, the concatenation of remembrances so intense she had felt the crunch of the sand under her bare feet, smelled the salt in the dark wind. She could not remember how long ago those images had been engraved on her brain, but it seemed to her that the unwelcome message she had read in the mirror must mean that it had been many years ago—but that was wrong: she should be able to remember when that vertiginous coming together of personal and cosmic drama had occurred, remember the exact date without even thinking about it. But there was only a blank.

Suddenly a burst of soft tones filled the room with pleasing harmonies, breaking into that worrying train of thought. Julia rose, slightly unsteadily, from her couch and activated the viewer. A man's face filled it; middle-aged, grey-moustached, thin hair combed carefully over the scalp. He smiled, a warm, genuine smile.

'Julia, my love! When will you grace our little soirée with your beauteous presence?'

Julia hesitated. She hadn't remembered accepting any invitation but there seemed to be so many things recently that she was unable to remember.

'Yes, Klaus,' she replied, speaking slowly as if using a language other than her mother tongue, 'yes, of course. Just a quick drink, I suppose?'

'What else? We all know you're far too busy with your demanding work for a long drink, my lovely temptress.'

Julia gave a mock frown.

'And what's wrong with a little work? You should try it sometime, Klaus!'

The man winced.

'Ouch! Julia, sweetheart, next time try using your scratching pole before using your claws. See you soon!'

The image vanished, but Julia remained in front of the screen, uncertain as to whether she wanted company or whether she just wanted to stay in the calm, warm embrace of her apartment. She shook her head abruptly. No! Company is what she needed to snap her out of this strange lethargy.

Suddenly Micky loped towards her and rubbed himself against her legs with almost human tenderness, interposing himself between her and the door as if trying to stop her from leaving. She stroked the animal perfunctorily and brushed past him, touching the door control. It opened silently, allowing mellow golden light to flood the room. The soft illumination struck the eyes of the monkey, turning them into phosphorescent discs of unfathomable amber light. The door closed, and the room became dim again, leaving the animal alone as a shadow among shadows.

***

Two valvar met in the noisome darkness of the Jovian afternoon. Not that it was dark to them, of course: their multifarious sensory organs, sensitive to all wavelengths from microwave to far ultraviolet, along with magnetic and other senses, effortlessly pierced the murk. They could sense the energies trapped in Jupiter's core, crushed under unimaginable pressure, and could feel the reassuring flood of infrared welling up like warm oil from that fearsome heat engine so far below. They could trace the lines of force in the planet's colossal magnetosphere, and see the tremendous current linking Io with its Cyclopean parent. Overhead they directly sensed the electric soprano of the lighting, the sad susurration of the aurorae, and overarching all, the strange cries of charged particles in the radiation belts—high-pitched and cavernous like cetacean calls resonating in dark Atlantic immensities. To the colonists, it was a near-perfect setting, a balmy interlude in the short Jovian afternoon.

They met on that mild, bright afternoon on the golden mirror of the warm hydrogen ocean, which, at this latitude, formed the temporary surface. Their mirrored hides glinted in the rainbow flashes of the pleasant lightning. They came closer: huge, streamlined, polished shapes that somehow radiated power and purpose, just as the lambent sky above them shone with the stored energy of its absorbed radiations. They met and touched antennae: terabytes of data passed between them at near lightspeed, and, in a seeming instant, whole libraries of information crossed between them; some of their poetry and song; some of their philosophies; some of their shared experiences in their unimaginably distant home galaxy; some of the details of their grand plan to remodel their adopted world, and much, much else.

'It is a pleasant world,' said the First, 'but sometimes I feel sad when I look around and think that we shall never see Sannakrann again and those we loved.'

'Yes, it is sad,' the Second said, 'yet this little world is good. At present, it is an empty wilderness, but we will make it a garden. One day it will be thronged with our kind, a closely woven planetary mind with trillions of denizens inhabiting every oceanic stratum down to the metallic zone. They will know no other homeland but this and will rejoice in its beauty. And then there will be this entire galaxy to mould and master; so many worlds like this to fill with our descendants until...'

'Until,' laughed the other, 'if our kin on Sannakrann ever discover us, they will wonder which is the backward colony and which is the metropolis!'

The idea delighted them, and, briefly, the hurtling terabits of information coalesced around the single vision of the Jovian colonisation.

'It is a tragedy we lost so many in the incident,' the First said, after an infinitesimally short pause.

'Yes, we will remember our friends…'

'We have grieved for them. I refer to the fact that we have fallen below the critical number of nodes for the Communicator, which in turn means we must work through the humans. You know I was against that.'

'Yes, dear friend, I know. But we cannot wait until new members come into being. Our hold here is precarious. Our bodies are not optimum for this low gravity. Working with the humans will save time—that could be crucial.'

The First lifted a few of its radiation sensors from the steaming hydrogen fluid just as a mass of metastable solid hydrogen burst up beside them. They ignored it. It could not harm them. Nothing could. To the First's many eyes the small disc of the Sun was just visible, encircled with haloes and dropping noticeably to the far-distant horizon under Jupiter's swift rotation.

'And what will we do with them when we are secure? They fear us deep inside. Their minds have thin shells of restraint over a core of violence and irrationality. Their world groans under its load of flesh and bone. In their blind chaos, many starve and die. As a race, they are deeply flawed—enough intelligence to suffer but not enough to solve their problems.'

'But of course: even we have not always been as we are now. In this universe, complexity evolves but slowly from simplicity. But now that we are here, we can spare them much misery. Their societies are proving easy to direct by simple psychological and biochemical procedures, but we have already begun to do more. Their genetic basis is extremely simple, and we can easily perform a few trivial manipulations which will adjust them in a way which will allow us to free them from their own stupidities and enable them to live in harmony with their tiny world and each other. Already we have closed down certain dangerous areas of their research which would have proved harmful to them.'

'I already know all of this, friend. Will they thank us? I doubt it.'

'They will not thank us, because they will be unaware we have changed them for the better. But what of that? We do not labour for reward. They will be happier with each passing year, and we will make their world a park for them to play in and be happy. Their content will be our reward—But enough of this chatter! The Sun is almost set, and you haven't given me that race you promised!'

'You're still crazy enough to measure yourself against the champion, are you?' roared the other, good-naturedly. At once, the two disengaged their antennae and hurled their sleek forms through the glutinous waves, the force of their exertions launching hydrogen spray dozens of metres into the air; no mean feat under the iron grip of the planet's gravity. They sped on toward the westering Sun, their wakes merging, blurring, dissolving. The Sun snapped out behind the mist-wreathed line of the incredibly distant horizon.

To human eyes—before those fragile organs were destroyed by the fierce environment—nothing would have been visible at all.

***

Julia sat down slowly on the cushioned chair, keeping her eyes fixed on the steaming mug of coffee throughout the manoeuvre. Only when she was sitting safely did she look up at her fellow workers. Marianne was there, as usual stroking her Himalayan colourpoint cat, an animal so richly endowed with fur that Julia estimated it made up some ninety per cent of the creature's body mass. Klaus was there, smiling crookedly at her over a large glass of wine; Raymond was staring out over the thronged lounge, his face almost expressionless but carrying a slight tinge of anxiety, Julia thought. She scolded herself inwardly: she was projecting her own feelings onto others again. Almost forcing herself to relax, she smiled at the two who were looking at her with welcoming expressions. She was now glad Klaus had called her; she had been spending too much time alone, too much time plugged into the great Valveren Communicator. Now she needed a dose of people, some harmless chat, some gossip, maybe an off-colour joke or two! The white noise of hundreds of conversations around her was soothing after the arid silence of her room.

'Well,' said Klaus, 'you finally got here. You know you're turning into quite a workaholic, Julia, my dear. You're putting the rest of us to shame.'

Julia raised the coffee mug in mock salutation.

'You took the words out of my mouth, Klaus.' And as he opened his mouth to carry on the banter, she went on: 'But surely you three must have found something to do recently?'

'Yes of course. We have been hard at work dealing with the problem of containing gravitational radiation, haven't we, Marianne?'

Marianne looked up from her cat for a moment, and cast a knowing glance in Julia's direction.

'Klaus, Julia's just teasing you again.'

Julia smiled gently. Marianne's voice was very realistic, with the correct overtones and phrasing, very much like her original voice had been, even down to the melodious soft French accent, before cancer had destroyed her larynx. The vocaliser she was using was a lightweight crown hidden within her waves of rich, golden hair—so unlike Julia's mousey brown. The vocaliser had been one of humanity's last inventions before the arrival of the Valveren had made human invention unnecessary. It needed no implants to pick up and amplify brain cell firings and convert them directly to speech. In fact, it didn't even need to be in actual contact with the cranium, being sensitive enough to do its work even a few centimetres away. It could also translate from one language to another without any noticeable delay, which was why vocalisers were ubiquitous among the multinational human contingent on Jupiter. One of humanity's last inventions—Julia frowned: why was that a slightly disturbing thought?

But Klaus was leaning towards her, dropping his voice conspiratorially to a stage whisper.

'You know all this brain work leaves the body in a state of extreme nervous tension. That can be very dangerous. So why don't you call round to my room afterwards and I'll show you that special intimate relaxation treatment I mentioned last week?'

'Oh Klaus,' breathed Julia, 'I'd just love to, but Marianne told me that when she tried it, she got so relaxed that she fell asleep!'

Klaus closed his eyes in mock pain as Marianne dug him in the ribs. Her vocaliser gave a giggle—just a little metallic, Julia thought.

Suddenly Raymond spoke. He did not turn to look at them, but continued to stare through the mass of crowded tables, through the riotous clusters of foliage and flowers, as if his gaze was penetrating the wall of the dome and continuing out into interplanetary space.

'I wonder what's happening on Earth,' he finally said.

The badinage stopped. Earth! It was as if someone had mentioned an ex-friend that everyone had agreed never to speak of again.

'Earth?' Klaus said the word as if learning to pronounce it. 'Earth? What made you think of that place?'

'I don't know.' Finally, Raymond turned to face them. 'I just found myself thinking this morning— of Earth.'

Klaus frowned.

'Well, I don't think anything is "happening"—as you put it. "Happening" implies struggle, conflict. I should think there's very little of that now, and everyone is glad of it. They're too busy learning all they need from the Valveren. With global peace and unlimited energy, all economic problems must vanish. When they go, politics just becomes administration. It used to be said that it was a misfortunate to be born in interesting times; well, from now on all times will be uninteresting and we'll all be the happier for it. Who wants all that striving, that insecurity? When something you have yearned for finally happens, there's always a sense of anti-climax. But that's a lot better than the alternative.'

Raymond nodded slowly, as if glad to be convinced.

'Yes, yes, of course. It's odd. I don't know why I suddenly thought about that place.' He relapsed into silence again.

'It's them who will be thinking about us,' Klaus went on, 'we hand-picked pioneers who, out of billions, had the chance to work directly with the Valveren. I'll bet our pictures are on every classroom wall!'

Work with the Valveren? thought Julia. *We must be very important.* She remembered her first absorption into the Communicator. It had been terrifying at first. But there were no terminals, no claustrophobic booths. One just pressed a button and one's room filled with a strange purplish light; a light which somehow one sensed directly in the brain itself rather than through the retinas. It was an ineffable experience: it could not be explained, only experienced. The Communicator short-circuited all sensory inputs, replacing them with images fed directly into older parts of the brain itself. On her first entry, she had found herself a disembodied consciousness adrift in a lambent sea of gentle light. Gradually the machine had trained her to recognise other human minds, to realise that she was linked up in a great network of being. Slowly she had understood that in some sense the individual minds were components of a mighty, intangible computer.

She had seen eldritch formulae and symbols appear before her, and, somehow, she had known what she must do. In communion with the others, she had manipulated those symbols, expanded, simplified, substituted terms, drawn inferences; done a myriad things that, when disconnected, she could no longer clearly remember, let alone explain. She had partaken of a higher level of consciousness, but her individual brain could hold no more than fragments of what her mentality had achieved. And there was a mystery: why did she feel as if her own conscious, reasoning powers were simply irrelevant to her tasks?

They had spent longer and longer periods within it, learning more about its awesome powers of harnessing intelligence—if that was indeed what it was doing. And she and a few others had learned that they were not alone. The portion of the Communicator they were embedded in was simply the lowest, crudest level: the Valveren themselves were in the highest levels and occasionally the reverberations of their usage could be sensed in the human level. The Communicator usually shielded them from direct contact, but on one occasion the Valveren must have been battling with a particularly intractable problem because the backwash from their level suddenly became a penetrating glare, as if an amateur astronomer had glimpsed the Sun for a terrible instant. The Communicator had been forced to disconnect them to save them from damage. And—and there was something else. Once, or maybe it was twice, she had felt a third presence in the Communicator—not the Valveren, not her fellow humans, but another entity, almost familiar but—not quite. Almost familiar, like a face in a crowd that stirs a memory that twists and turns and will not be dragged into the light. And then it is gone.

Julia shuddered suddenly, as if her coffee had become unendurably bitter; once again, she could feel the weight of her situation, almost like directly experiencing the gigatonnes of churning Jovian gases that were pressing from all sides onto their domes. So why did the others not feel it?

She started, forcing herself out of an oneiric daze. Suddenly she realised that there had been silence for some time. The mug of coffee was quite cold, and she put it on the table, feeling foolish.

'Klaus, I'm not sure any more. Is what we do any use to them? None of us here are really scientists. I was an Interior Designer, for God's sake. So why are we here on this hell planet?'

Klaus had stopped looking at her. The amity had drained from his face. He was brushing at the seams of his trousers and seemed absorbed in the activity.

'Julia, perhaps you're thinking of your own problems too much. Perhaps you should be slightly more grateful for your immense privilege of being here on this marvellous world, which for most of humanity will never be more than a speck of light. Now, at last, we are moving towards the climax of the Valveren's work on Jupiter.'

'Yes, the climax,' echoed Julia. Her voice was little more than a whisper. Yet it carried authority; as one, the other three leaned slightly towards her.

'Then the Valveren will always be with us. Looking after us. Ensuring we don't do anything foolish or childish.'

And then it came to her—the central paradox burst into her mind like a nuclear flash blazing up into an astounded sky.

She fixed all three of them with a steely glare.

'You three, you happy three. Tell me this: how long have we been here, on Jupiter!'

***

Two valvar met in the smoking mists of the Jovian evening. Above them the folded banners of aurorae danced in kaleidoscopic hues, mixing and merging into each other in playful excitement. Argent Europa stood at the zenith, a silver coin glimpsed through a smudged lens.

The two made contact. Cataracts of information flowed between them. Among those Niagaras of data, there were many separate flows: one was concerned with their great project.

'I feel impatient,' said the Third. 'We are so close.'

'Yes, I share your feelings,' the Fourth replied, 'Soon, it will be complete, and we will swim through the oceans of a second Sannakrann. Then we can turn our energies outwards, on to the next step in our remaking of this galaxy.'

The other did not take up the theme and seemed a little hesitant.

'Yet, I have calculated there is a danger in the project, my friend. There is a cusp in the energy distribution beyond which it must go to completion. Once though that point, it cannot be stopped or reversed. I have already broadcast this on the Communicator, but few seemed interested. I would like you to examine the proof.'

Instantly in the other's mind there appeared a three-dimensional matrix of conditional probabilities. The second valvar tested the initial set of assumptions and found the set to be consistent. It transformed them into a series of partial differential equations, which it instantly solved, and then made the necessary substitutions to the variables.

'Yes indeed; a cusp beyond which there is no return. Hardly unexpected and hardly significant. We will operate at much lower energies than you seem to be assuming. And why should we want to return through the cusp? A new Sannakrann awaits us on the other side!'

The Third took a long time—by Valveren standards—to reply.

'I am not sure. You are correct in that the issue seems academic, yet there is something about this project that disturbs me. We have set it up in haste, left out automatic safety checks—and there is a totally new, untested set of variables—the humans …'

'The humans!' The other was slightly censorious. 'I agree that it is unfortunate that we must use them, but how could they be a problem? We know them down to their mitochondria.'

'A slight exaggeration but I take the point. Their reactions are very predictable. It…' Once again the other hesitated, 'it must be this coming apotheosis. Too much cerebration and too little physical activity perhaps.'

'Easily remedied, you bookworm!' laughed the Fourth, 'Come, let's see if you can match my diving record, or indeed'—and the laughter grew arch—'come anywhere near it!'

The Third spluttered in mock anger and then the two mighty beings turned gracefully and plunged deep into the sweet-smelling waves.

***

'How long have we been here?'

Marianne's vocaliser failed to reproduce the puzzlement her mind must have been registering. Instead, her gaze was directed down at her cat, which she was stroking continually in an oddly mechanical fashion. 'What is that question supposed to mean?'

'Exactly what I said.'

Julia sensed a nightmarish feeling that she was struggling to the surface through layer after layer of cotton wool.

'I looked in the mirror a while ago and a middle-aged woman looked back at me. I'd never seen her before! I don't remember being middle-aged. In fact, I'm not exactly sure how old I am, although I'm pretty sure I'm under forty. And I don't remember how long I've been on Jupiter. All I remember is that we all arrived together. So, I repeat: how long have we been on Jupiter!'

Marianne seemed about to speak but returned to looking at her cat. Klaus sat in a frozen fashion as if wrestling with some internal conflict. Only Raymond seemed normal.

'Yes, yes,' he said very slowly, 'how long? It must be two or three years.'

It was Julia's turn to go momentarily silent and rigid. She felt her heart lurch.

'Three years? But that's impossible. It must be longer than that.'

Klaus stirred, his conflict resolved. He looked angry.

'Julia, I think that's enough. This is getting ridiculous. What do you think we are here—some collection of amnesiac Rip Van Winkles or something? What does it matter if we've been here three years or thirty! We're doing our part in the greatest project human beings have ever been involved in!'

Julia felt her own anger rising, and the emotion was almost new to her. A tiny part of her mind realised that she had not had a strong emotion for a long time; the adrenal glands had nearly forgotten how to pump out their hormones.

'*The greatest project!* She almost spat the words. 'We don't even know what it is! How can our work be of any significance to the Valveren? If you were designing a new logic circuit would you subcontract it to a baboon! Whatever they want us for it's not our knowledge!'

Klaus looked too angry to speak. Marianne continued to stare glumly at her cat which at long last was trying to escape the incessant stroking. Yet Raymond still seemed to be able to calmly discuss things with her.

'But, Julia, our work in the Communicator; the equations we see and solve…'

'But we don't do that, at least at the conscious level. I don't know much more about advanced mathematics than that damned cat does. We are taken into that thing; we are used by it; turned into living microprocessors by it, but at a level below our ordinary consciousness. I think it doesn't matter one single damn what our backgrounds or abilities are, even our basic intelligence. That thing needs a certain number of processing nodes, and for some reason it doesn't have enough and we…'

'That's enough!'

The shout was enough to make heads turn many tables away. Klaus stood over her, his face literally purple with rage. Spittle foamed in the corners of his mouth. The distant, analytical portion of Julia's mind noted that this was the first time she had actually seen a real-life purple face. Was the man having some kind of attack?

But Klaus continued: 'We've had enough of this gibberish from you! It's—it's …' His head turned from side to side as he sought for the word, 'It's *blasphemous!* Get out, get out; we don't want to hear any more of this shit! Go on—get out!'

Julia looked up at the madman with both fear and amazement. Too much was happening, too quickly for her rusted reflexes. She got up unsteadily, backing away at the same time. Surely every head was now turned towards her, every eye piercing the very soul of this peculiar woman who was causing so much trouble. She turned and walked away, never daring to meet the gaze of those she passed. It was not until she was out of the leisure area that her pace returned to normal. Then she stopped, leaning against the curved wall of the corridor, feeling the whole complex whirl giddily around and around, with her as the axis. She could still hear the featureless hum of their chatter babbling around her; every sound, she knew, was to do with her.

She hurried through the winding innards of the Valveren complex and rushed into her own apartment, gratefully sinking into her chair. She sat there, her head in her hands, feeling a sudden need to be hugged and comforted, to rest her head on a hard shoulder and to feel a hand stroking her hair.

How long had it been!

She looked for Micky, but he was nowhere to be seen. That was unusual, she thought. He could work the door release, but usually, they went out together. Where was he? She put her hand to her brow, and suddenly there was a hot wetness on her cheeks. Her eyes seemed to burn as if, once again, long unused channels were being forced back into operation. Finally, she leaned back in the chair, and her lips formed a name they had not spoken for an unknown time.

'Carlo,' she whispered, 'Where are you, my love?'

***

'You little bitch!'

Marianne looked down in amazement at the blood oozing from the claw marks on her skin. Her cat made a spitting noise and backed away into a corner. Marianne lowered the arm she had raised to strike and sat down instead, dabbing at the injured hand. The cat was probably not to blame; the animal had little time to itself and had presumably grown tired of the continual petting she gave it. Still, it had been behaving decidedly oddly recently, prowling back and forth as if trying to find something.

Marianne leaned back, blowing soft, blond strands from her eyes. Everything seemed to be going wrong lately, and that dreadful scene in the leisure area had upset her dreadfully. Everyone appeared to be on edge as if the springs of their lives had been wound too tightly. And in the back of her own mind, she sensed some unease as if a long-repressed worry was trying to insinuate itself back into her consciousness.

Gradually she allowed herself to drift into the release of sleep, forgetting the day's disturbances. Slowly her breathing grew deep and regular.

The cat lay still, watching her, its eyes discs of green phosphorescence in the warm gloom. Then suddenly it moved, jumping to the couch by the door and, stretching full-length, it pressed the door release. There, silhouetted in the rectangle of light that was revealed, stood the one who had been expected. He came in, the door sliding softly shut.

***

Julia found herself rising through the resistant strata of sleep, back to an unwelcome wakefulness. The short Jovian night was long past, but that was irrelevant: they followed the standard Terrestrial day and night cycle within the domes. To a human, of course, it would always be black outside, darker than any Earthly night could ever be, except when the blazing forks of the fearsome lightning flashed.

Julia felt reluctant to return to consciousness; this sleep was preferable to reality. But after lying quietly for a while, she opened her eyes slowly to see once again her over-familiar apartment, the same sight that had—with a few exceptions, now best forgotten—greeted her on every previous awakening. She stretched half-heartedly and flinging back the sheet started to swing her legs off of the bed.

She did not complete the movement. She was not alone! There was a presence in the room, she knew. She felt a slight stirring of the fine hairs on the back of her neck: there was something with her, something strange and yet familiar. It was like the feeling she had had when absorbed in the communal mind of the Communicator. The sleep now thoroughly drained from her, she stood up slowly, glancing quickly around the room. All seemed normal, the soft tinkle of the fountain, the cool air from the air conditioning nipping gently at her toes.

There! By the table, a shadow moved. She tensed into a crouched position, her left hand reaching out for a statuette to wield as a weapon. The shadow moved into the light. It was Micky.

'Micky!' she cried, stretching out her arms, 'you little bastard, why did you give me such a fright! Come here!'

She stopped. Micky was somehow different; his posture was more erect, his gaze more direct—and he was carrying Marianne's vocaliser!

'Mick…'. The words died in her throat. The monkey met her gaze steadily, looking directly up at her with brown eyes that gripped her with seeming hypnotic power.

The vocaliser spoke. The voice was still mainly Marianne's but distorted like an old-fashioned radio broadcast drifting in and out of a weak signal.

'Hello, Julia. It's good to speak to you again.'

Julia didn't know if she fainted or not. There seemed to be a part of her memory cut out: she didn't remember sitting on the bed, but there she was, and the monkey's face was almost on a level with hers and its horrible leathery fingers were intertwined with her own. Its face came close and she smelled the animal breath. Somehow, she had never noticed that before.

Is this what she had felt coming on these last few days, she wondered, still able to summon up a detached, analytical portion of her mind even in the face of screaming madness.

She knew how her insanity would develop: first, she would see talking animals, then talking furniture, taps dripping blood. There would be doctors standing around, pitying her while she muttered to herself and pulled out handfuls of hair. This was only Stage One. After that, there would be no escape.

The monkey touched her face, trying to turn it to force her to look straight at him. She came back to life and violently pushed the creature away. It hit the wall and slid to the floor. In an instant, she had found the statuette and stood over him, her arm swinging up in an arc which it would retrace to deliver the killing blow. The monkey looked up passively, holding the vocaliser in its little paws.

'Julia,' the crackling voice said, 'you must listen. I don't want to hurt you. I'm no threat to you. Nor,' the creature added, apparently guessing her thoughts, 'are you mad.'

Julia dropped the statuette and found herself slumping to the floor beside the monkey. She forced herself into a sitting position but could not look at the animal.

'Monkeys can't speak,' she said thickly, as much to herself as to anyone else, 'even with a vocaliser. And you tell me I'm not mad. This bloody place has driven me mad!' A terrible thought struck her. 'Christ, I'm probably not even on Jupiter! That's part of my delusion!'

'Julia! You've got to listen to me! You've got to believe what I say; there's so little time!'

Julia shrugged.

'Well whatever you are, you're not afraid of clichés.' She turned slightly but still did not quite look at him. 'So what are you, Micky? A Jovian, a leprechaun or a badly digested cheese sandwich?'

She took deep breaths between every other word. It seemed to help: perhaps this was not insanity after all. But if it was not—what was it?

'What am I? Julia, do you remember that time we stopped the boat to watch the humpbacks go past and used the hydrophone to listen to them reciting their poetry to each other?'

Now she turned to look askance at the monkey. A tremendous pressure suddenly seemed to detonate in her skull; she felt nausea, elation, agony; she felt emotions, for which there are no words, swell up in a surge that in one more instant would destroy her.

'I am Carlo,' the monkey said.

The window was transparent. There was no sound, but outside the Jovian lightning raved, a jagged scimitar of feral energy, blue-white, elemental, ineluctable, unendurable.

'You are Carlo.'

'I am his—mental essence. I am his neurological pattern impressed on the brain of this monkey. It was my field of research, surely you remember?'

Julia looked obliquely at the animal. This was a sick joke—no, it was an obscene joke played on her by God Himself. It was an obscenity so vile that she must destroy this mockery of humanity, rend the furred limbs from…

'Julia!' The mechanical voice now carried authority. It was as if … 'Think!—I beg you! You know my research as a neurophysiologist; you know that I had proved it possible and had begun the first experiments.'

Her hands were making little scrabbling motions. Her gaze darted everywhere but would not—could not—fix on that face, so close to a human but so unutterably distant.

'Yes, yes,' she muttered, 'yes, but with animals, only animals. Medical ethics for God's sake—to do it to a human, to do it to yourself, to put your mind into the filthy brain of a bloody monkey, to…'

'So you think I did it as some kind of student prank, do you, Julia? Do you think I said: "Hey, let's put my mind into a monkey for a few laughs!" Do you! We did it because we thought the future of the whole of humanity hung on our actions!'

Julia never realised until that moment she could be so strong. She took the howling pressure on her mind and calmed it. She drove the pain from her body by sheer force of will.

The two remained silent for some minutes as her muscles gradually unknotted. Then, when she knew she was finally ready, she lifted her head; she lifted her head and looked directly at the monkey.

'Carlo, is it really you? Can it be you inside that creature?'

'It is me. My God, Julia, you can't even begin to guess the hell of it! The nightmare of waking up in this body, the loneliness of being in the same room as you day after day, not able to touch you, to kiss you, to talk to you, to share my fears. And those times you would hold me, the times you would stroke me …God, Julia, it's me that's mad! Mad to have done it and ten times madder with what it's done to me!'

'But Carlo, you said that when you were working on this that it wasn't stable, the brain from one species couldn't indefinitely support the thought patterns of another, that, that—it would revert!'

'Revert. Yes. I'm one of the lucky ones. It wasn't thought that many primates could be used. To have everyone turn up in this base with a monkey would have alerted minds even less able than the Valveren. Chimpanzees would have been best, but they don't make good pets. The monkey brain was the best we could hope to use. It has held the pattern for quite some time. I estimate the loss of function as only thirty percent. But the others…'

'The others!' Julia gasped, 'you mean all the other animals…'

'Ah, you never wondered that so many of your colleagues were animal lovers.' If the monkey could have smiled wryly, it would have done so. 'We are not as clever as our masters, but we still have some psychological techniques. We nudged many (but not all of course) of those destined for Jupiter to become animal lovers, even if they had never previously owned as much as a hamster. The Valveren accepted their servants' affection for animals as a normal part of human behaviour. But cat and dog brains do not hold the pattern so well. I'm nearly alone now. Nearly.'

It seemed now that nothing could reach her. She heard her own voice discuss this collection of absurdities calmly, coolly.

'So you and some others had their minds copied and transferred to the brains of domestic animals. Seems perfectly reasonable; after all, it happens all the time. But may I ask why?'

'The Valveren, of course. It was clear to many of us that their arrival had altered humanity's future forever. In only the first few weeks after they appeared, they had solved every problem of planetary mismanagement that we had been fumbling around with. They gave us safe, inexhaustible energy. They gave the world a central Database that contained the answer to every scientific question we'd ever asked. EVERY question. Science died that day.

'Mathematics died the day after. We rushed to find the questions that always eluded us. Polydimensional topology, P=NP, Riemann Hypothesis, the relation of mathematics to physical reality, and many this vocaliser can't pronounce. Soon we were left with problems with which we could understand the conclusions, but not the proofs. And then when those were gone, we were left with problems where we couldn't even understand the question!'

Julia sat up straighter. Still, she held the gaze of this man/monkey, hallucination/nightmare.

'And so what! The Valveren are cleverer than we are. Don't you think that most people come across others that are smarter than they are? I know I have. Good God, is that all this is—pique at not being top of the class, king of your own personal dung heap!'

'No, no, it's much more than that. When you meet people cleverer than you are, you know they share the same quest as you, that there are fields of endeavour which you can explore together——maybe as an assistant rather than as team leader—but together. But now we know that whatever layer of discovery we peel away, to an endless depth, the Valveren have already been there and mastered it. If our greatest minds toiled for a thousand years, we would have no more than the smallest fragment of what we can get in a simple retrieval from their Database. All that we could have discovered with brains that took from the caves is already there, waiting to be printed out at the touch of a button. Human history is over.'

'Human history is not over until there are no more humans. Human life is more than science, more than mathematics. Human life is interaction with other people; joy in those—in those,'—she gagged momentarily—'in those you love: friends, family, children; in personal, not racial, triumphs. This is Master Race gibberish!'

'You think so, do you? We all know the Valveren are not monsters. They do not want to eat us, enslave us, or rape our women. They are a glorious race; more so than we know, more than we can imagine, for all we have seen of them is this one small, lost scouting party. But somewhere out there is their true civilisation; one so powerful, so nearly Godlike, that they will harm us just through being what they are; without intending to, without even knowing that they are doing so; just as you are ignorant of the fate of the mites that live in your eyelashes. We did not consult the wolves when we turned them into lapdogs. They will not consult us on our future. They know what is best for us.'

Julia snorted.

'The words of a bloodless academic, Carlo. Maybe you're not Carlo. Maybe I'm just talking to the vocaliser. A bloodless machine.'

The vocaliser made an odd sound which Julia eventually interpreted as a sigh.

The monkey/Carlo spoke again.

'Before we made this decision, which so horrifies you, there were clear indications that they had already begun to intervene in human affairs—oh, benevolently, of course! Certain world trouble spots that had been simmering since the last century suddenly cleared up, but not for any obvious reason that we could see. Nothing had apparently changed, but people who had always hated each other suddenly stopped doing so. Just like that.'

'Then good for the Valveren! Perhaps we don't deserve them if that's our response to good news. You obviously prefer burning napalm to world peace.'

'We were gradually solving those problems. We were learning to live together. We got through the Twentieth Century, didn't we? Only just, but we got through it. Don't you see that those incidents show that the Valveren have the power to control us in subtle, invisible ways? Alter our mental states, our ways of thinking!'

'So, they want to turn us into peace-loving sheep. But we'll be happy sheep!'

The monkey turned its brown eyes, somehow sad-looking, up to stare deeply into hers.

'Then there were the virus vectors that appeared shortly after.'

'Virus vectors?'

'It's an old technique for inserting foreign genes into genotypes. But these vectors weren't ours. We discovered them by chance in people who showed no sign of any infections. We discovered that they were injecting genes into our DNA structures. Genes clearly human, but unknown, artificial genes, created purely to be incorporated into us, carrying characteristics that we can only guess at.'

'No doubt for love, altruism. We'd have done the same if we'd been clever enough.'

'Would we, I wonder? But would we have done it without telling the recipients! The Valveren see us as things to be controlled for our own good. Set the human thermostat at an optimum value and forget it! And those characteristics you find so admirable: love, altruism; very nice, but also included in the package are passivity, acceptance, docility!'

Julia said nothing. She felt a confused anger beginning to swell in her. It was wrong what the Valveren were doing, but was it so bad? Far better to accept it and live in contentment.

'And then finally,' the voice continued, still drifting in and out of clarity, 'we come to you people here; here on Jupiter. Why are you here?'

Julia started.

'Have you been putting those thoughts in my mind?'

'Of course, my love. Just think it through, Julia, why would such beings as the Valveren need human help in their project? There's nothing brilliant about the people here. Even those who are trained scientists are just middle rankers. They're just making up the numbers.'

'The numbers?'

'Yes. It's partly guesswork, but I think the Communicator works best above a critical number of processing nodes. It's biomechanical in a similar way to the Valveren themselves. They lost two of their number in whatever accident brought them here. The number of human brains here roughly indicates the ratio between their brains and ours.'

'But how can you know all this?' She suddenly fell silent and then blurted: 'It was you I sensed in the Communicator!'

'Yes, although there were others with me, at least initially. And unlike the everyday humans here, we sent our best: logicians, mathematicians, computer scientists. We think—we hope—that we operated unseen. The Valveren knew that any human in the Communicator would be under their control, so we believe—we think—that they did not distinguish us from the rest of you.'

Julia did not let that word go unnoticed.

'Control?'

'Control, Julia, my love. They didn't want human irrationality and emotions getting in the way of their project. So they suppressed significant features of your personality before you arrived: curiosity, willpower and, mercifully, fear of this terrible planet. Humans can't remain sane knowing they're trapped at the bottom of thousands of kilometres of choking gases. Knowing that only a metal skin is saving them from instant annihilation. Those suppressed feelings are what I've been trying to reawaken when we are together in the Communicator.'

'But you weren't conditioned?'

'No, why condition a monkey? That was the whole reason for this crazy subterfuge! But I've been caught in a trap far more frightening than Jupiter. Perhaps that has driven me around in a circle to sanity again. But Julia, I must hurry. The end is close, and I must anticipate your questions. When we had formed our suspicions of what was happening to our race, we knew that we had to spy on the Valveren. I nearly went mad when you volunteered to go to Jupiter—I promise I did not manoeuvre that—but then I knew I had to do my own volunteering. We knew that the volunteers would be controlled by some procedure, so, as I said, we arranged for as many as possible to take a mammalian pet with them. Each pet contained the imprinted mind of a specialist. Once we arrived, we used our anonymity to learn all we could. The Communicator was the key—without it we would not have gotten very far. Because entry was made easy for humans, it was easy for we companions, sitting patiently in the same room, to enter as well. We did so—hopefully, we were too minor a variable to rouse suspicions. We observed you; we also observed the Valveren from a great distance. And in the last few days, we have worked out what the Valveren are doing here. It wouldn't normally have taken so long, but our minds are decaying, reverting to the animal. Thoughts are muddy these days—so muddy. We just hope and pray enough of our abilities have survived for our conclusions to be right. If not…'

He paused, and looked around as if he was hoping for some reassurance; from someone, somewhere.

But there was none.

He returned to looking up at the being who had once been his wife. His eyes, animal though they were, showed a great sadness.

'We believe they have two strands to their project. They don't know how they got here or how to contact their home worlds. But they will! Maybe sometime in the next few minutes, they will send a message to that great civilisation: Here we are! Come and join us in this empty galaxy!

'But there is another part of the plan. To defeat that, we must have real humans, free from conditioning. So for the past two months, I have been reaching out to you while we were both in the Communicator, trying to loosen the chains on your mind. And whether or not I have fully succeeded, I had to reveal myself to you.'

'Why,' said Julia dully, 'why is it so urgent now?'

'The second part of the project is only a day or so from completion,' replied Carlo/Micky. 'The Valveren are colonising Jupiter, we all know that. But Jupiter is not ideal for them. Their home planet is even more massive than this one, so Jupiter to them is like Mars would be to us. But they have the power to alter planetary environments. They are going to collapse the radius of this world, increasing its density so that the gravity at the mean oceanic surface will rise: we think to about three and a half gravities. Then Jupiter will be perfect for them; they will populate it, embark on the colonisation of this galaxy and one day, maybe in a million years, maybe tomorrow, contact their home worlds. And what of humanity, Julia?'

'What of it?'

'We will be gone. Evaporated. We can't coexist with beings such as these. They burn too bright for we fragile moths; we cannot endure them.'

'But even if they were to go away, their home worlds will still find us one day.'

'One day, yes. But the universe is vast, vast beyond our comprehension. The Valveren have told us that they were thrown here by accident. Their main civilisation could search for them galaxy by galaxy, each galaxy being scanned in a heartbeat, and still take them ten million years to find us! Only if the ones marooned here find a way of contacting the home world would that time be short.'

'Ten years or ten million years, the result will be the same.'

The monkey leapt forward to grasp her wrists. She did not resist.

'We can't make that decision for our descendants. We have to hope and do what we can do now!'

'Descendants!' Julia laughed bitterly. 'Yes, always in the abstract, never the inconvenient flesh, eh Carlo?' A thought which had been festering in her subconscious suddenly burst into clarity. 'The pattern transfer—it's based on a copy of the neuronic pattern. A copy. That means the original Carlo is still going about his business back on Earth, having a wonderful time with all those women that used to worship him, knowing nothing about you and caring less. Knowing nothing about you, his— his offspring. His only son a monkey and identical twin at the same time!'

'Julia, what you say is true, but none of that matters any more. I am as much Carlo as the one who stayed. I am Carlo. One day I went to sleep with electrodes taped to my scalp, and when I awoke, I was in the body of this animal. And I did it for what?— for an abstraction, for the sake of my species, for my people. You thought you had a hard-luck story to tell, did you, Julia! Don't you realise that I did it knowing that there was no way back! Even if my mind could be restored and recopied, where would it go? The original is still in possession!'

'Then humankind is finished,' said Julia, 'we can't expel the Valveren any more than we could carry Jupiter off on our shoulders.'

'No, there is a chance, just one, last chance. One chance, and if that fails, nothing. We spied and eavesdropped when we were in the Communicator. Earth's finest minds battled against the steady loss of their abilities to listen and understand. We overheard a debate about their project. There is one element of vulnerability that comes from their reliance on human brains. The Communicator is the hub of it all—it has absolute control of the project because of the magnitude of the forces required and the electronic speed with which they must be controlled. Even the Valveren must rely on machines more able than they are. And for this one brief moment, the Communicator needs the human minds embedded in it.'

'And as you're telling me all this, I must have some role to play.'

'One mind that is aware, yes. Yours is the only mind that we, I, have managed to free from the conditioning. In the Communicator, your mind is merged with the other humans, and that fusion forms the base on which the Valveren superstructure rests. At the midpoint of the project, data packages—call them "parameters"—will be passed to you and at that instant you are the first link in the human chain. You must alter those parameters. You will be the only truly conscious individual in that chain, and you alone will be aware of what you are doing.'

'And then the Valveren will realise that we can't be domesticated and go somewhere else.'

'No. They will die. They have to die. It is the only way we can be certain they will not make contact with their home world. But in order to be certain of that, all of us on Jupiter must die: humans, Valveren, talking monkeys—all gone. But even if we succeed there are grave dangers to humanity in our plan: when the gases are compressed there will be a vast adiabatic increase in temperature. But not enough to initiate fusion—we are certain of that, at least. However, our plan will destabilise the asteroid belt. But those who have become newly freed on Earth will have to handle that; we have known how to deflect space rocks for some time.' Carlo paused. 'Julia, it's strange but the outcome will be like the last few lines in the Knight's Tale—remember how I used to quote the modern English version? "Jupiter, the king/ Prince and cause of everything/ Converting all things back into the source/ From which they were derived, to which they course." And once our owners have gone, after a period of turmoil, of near disaster, humankind will recover from its brief contact with these aliens. Our people will destroy the Database, and we will go back to our own ways of discovery, our own mistakes, driving our own lives, forgetting our master's lap.'

'And you expect me to die for that? That we will be allowed to go back to our old, mad ways? You're only a smudged copy. I'm the real deal, Julia, the one and only. There's no backup of me stored safely somewhere!'

'Julia, do you think that the Valveren have your interests at heart, that they could even know what those interests might be? They can cross intergalactic space in a heartbeat, but the needs of a human being, of a woman, they cannot understand.

I've seen you look in the mirror; I've seen you study your face. The Communicator does that to people, Julia; it demands too much of our flimsy bodies. The damage it has done to your tissues is irreversible. It is unstoppable.

'Julia, you have been on Jupiter for eleven short months. And you are just twenty-seven years old. Your decay is not merely unstoppable—it is terminal.'

They sat there for several minutes more, in complete silence. Then, at last, Julia reached out her arms to the little crouching form opposite her. The monkey came to her and they kissed.

***

Julia had never before been absorbed into the Communicator in an uncontrolled state. It was frightening at first as she was instantly aware of the other minds crowding in upon her. Some she could recognise—there was Marianne, Klaus, yes—there was Raymond, and others she knew less well; they were all there. And for the first time, she could sense the Valveren's control on them, the taste of a grey sickness flowing from her companions as an indicator of what they had become—no longer fully human, merely vehicles of flesh needed only for their neurons. Yet this had been done without evil, simply the unheeded consequence of the gulf between the two races. Beyond, far beyond, she could detect the thoughts of the Valveren like a hidden sun suffusing the clouds. There was a palpable exhilaration in their mental network; even the great Valveren could be moved to boyish excitement now that their great world-sculpting enterprise neared its climax. And there, too, was Carlo. He had joined her. There was no greyness associated with his mind but a sense of fading, like a bulb still shining after the current had been removed. Sometimes his thoughts would dim to the point of extinction and then briefly flare up again. The beast was reclaiming its body.

Julia knew that soon, whatever happened, they would all be dead, used up by the demands of the superhuman on the merely human. A grim acceptance now flooded her whole being. And what of the Valveren? Had they solved the mystery of death as they had solved every other? It would make no difference now, for soon they would be hurled into its maw like the humblest mayfly.

Julia became aware that an image was being relayed to all the inhabitants of the Communicator. Gradually it took shape in her mental space until it became clear. Seemingly a few metres before her, the great world of Jupiter itself hung in space, brilliantly lit by the still-powerful Sun. She could see the ochre and brown bands of the swirling cloud belts, the orange stare of the Great Red Spot, staring angrily out like an inflamed Cyclopean eye. More than that, she could sense the Jovian lightning bolts, feel the concussion of their thunders. This must be something of how the Valveren perceived their adopted planet.

To slay such beings!

She forced her gaze back to the image of Jupiter. Now as she became more familiar with the properties of the mental projection, she could see the finer detail. In particular, she noticed that the planet seemed laced through with bright meridians of circulating forces that spanned the great globe from pole to pole. She realised that she was seeing engineering on a truly colossal scale: the Valveren had encased Jupiter in a network of invincible energies that would soon compress the planetary bulk until it produced a gravitational potential equal to that of their home world. For a moment, she felt a surge of both awe and love for these transcendent beings who were capable of such soaring triumphs of the will and intellect.

Carlo's mind was with her again.

'We will be together soon.'

'How odd,' thought Julia, 'do you duplicate the soul when you duplicate minds? Will one day another Carlo come to claim me?'

And then suddenly—it started.

She felt the urgent demands for mental resources lance down at her from the Valveren levels. The human minds meshed smoothly into one unit, providing both processing ability and, more importantly, volition to the higher levels. A smooth unit—but with one lonely component with its own volition.

Watch for the parameter, Carlo had said, *take it, alter it, pass it to the others; they will amplify it, blindly pass it on just as the terrible energies that Valveren have unleashed pass through the cusp!*

Julia sensed the world-moulding might of the Valveren machines building up, building up, up into a clonic paroxysm of force incredible.

There, there was the key parameter! Desperately, she focused, desperately she changed it, exhausted she passed it to the others who flung it on into other inexorable command chains.

In domes far removed from the humans, the great Valveren engines thundered into life. But their thunder did not settle into a calm, contented hum. No, it continued to increase in volume and pitch as the engines began to grapple with a massive overload.

The vast flows of power fountained onward, through the cusp. Now not even a deity could bid them return. Mounting to an orgasmic peak, irresistible energies grasped Jupiter and prepared to compress it like clay between Titanic hands. The gravitational potential of the new world would, almost instantly, leap to the new value: but now not to three and one half gravities.

No, now to *three hundred and fifty gravities*— transcendentally stronger than the Sun!

Under that inconceivable, monstrous, sledgehammering blow, flesh and bone would flow like water; every known material would instantly collapse into a monomolecular film, sweeping away machines and pets and humans and Valveren, crushing their atoms together in featureless ruin.

In the great domes, a terrible silence fell as the screams of the tortured machines became ultrasonic.

'Carlo, will it be worth it, all this destruction?'

'Ah, Julia, my love, unanswerable questions to the end.'

Julia's mind reeled as the apotheosis approached.

'Death,' she thought, 'what is it like?'

She thought no more: the great collapse began.

THE WAY BACK

When a fusion reactor fails catastrophically, the results are—well, catastrophic.
Fusion requires temperatures of about 100 million kelvins so that the matter is in its fourth state—plasma.

When that plasma is released in a sudden detonation without any attempt to reduce the pressure, the heat is enough to vaporise rock. There is also the concomitant release of fast neutrons, unfailingly deadly to any organic being unfortunate enough to be in range. But normally, as the quantities of hydrogen isotopes involved are not large, any escape of plasma would have simply local effects.

However, if the fusion reactor failed because a one-kiloton fission bomb went off nearby, this is no longer the case.

Only one man appeared to have survived the fission blast, and he was at a distance of five kilometres from the centre of the two combined cataclysms.

One man—Manuel Gonzales of Australasian Intelligence.

The blast was visible as a terrible, electric blue flash, fringed at the edges with sulfur-yellow, rapidly rising, darkening, and enfolding into the dread mushroom shape. It was followed by a furnace wind that tore up the charcoaled trees by their ashened roots and scattered the resultant dust across the sky. Yet one man, apparently, survived.

How?

He was meant to survive. At the moment when the hell of berserker atomic particles and hard radiation were unleashed, he was underground in a lead-lined concrete box, two metres by three, clad in an antiradiation suit.

An hour passed.

One and a half.

A small periscope edged up out of the charred ground and quickly surveyed the cadaver that had once been a New Guinean islet. After fifteen more minutes, the grey soil heaved, and a strange, nightmarish form emerged, reminiscent of a cockchafer escaping from its underground nursery. It stood as tall as a man but glinted silver in the unnaturally reddened sunlight. Its suit contained alumino-titanium fibres over a fluorocarbon base. Its head was a metal box with a silica faceplate, darkened by infused lead. Its hands were gleaming pincers that suddenly flexed like the claws of a crab. It began to move, but not as a man would, for the lead-heavy fabrics made the suit too heavy for human muscles, even when they belonged to a powerful individual like its current owner. It moved in a series of hops driven by a column of quivering gases thrusting from a cylinder on the creature's back.

The hops were five-metre arcs, rapidly crossing the calcined grey and black landscape as if purposely seeking some elusive quarry. Then it slowed as if that quarry were close.

Gonzales—for it was indeed he—then threw himself onto the murdered ground and waited.

Although alone—he was not alone.

Others were seeing what he saw. His retinas were connected to a transducer woven into his suit, and that complex creation amplified the signal and beamed a tight microwave up to a waiting satellite. From there, it was beamed again to a hidden complex where great brains studied full-colour, three-dimensional images. These were displayed on screens showing the same grim scene Gonzales himself was seeing.

'They are near,' C3 said.

'Obviously,' A0 replied curtly. 'The islet is too small for them to be anywhere else and have survived.'

C3 did not reply: there was no point in crossing swords with A0, and returned to studying what Gonzales was seeing.

Out of the ground not too far in front of Gonzales, a thin black periscope had risen, and, just as Gonzales' device had, it rotated a full 360, its field of view passing just above the watchful man as he lay behind a blistered ridge. Having shown nothing to alarm its operator, it withdrew. Gonzales changed to a crouching position—even through the bulky suit, he looked like a taut predator about to pounce.

The ground where the periscope had been heaved and a large slab slid away, revealing a deep rectangular pit of unknown depth, out of which came four figures, clad in suits similar to, but not identical with, that worn by their watcher. They all made cursory glances around, but, given the Gehenna that they observed, it must have seemed to them that they were only living creatures on the murdered islet.

They were, of course, wrong.

In the middle part of the Twenty-First century humanity had not become more peaceful. The tensions inherent in Earth's unstable political situation sought release as each group sought to dominate, rather than co-operate.

The swarming mass of Chinese, determined to regain the pre-eminence of the Middle Kingdom over the barbarians; the Sunni and the Shia, both equally resolute that their version of the Prophet's words would prevail; the African countries, still seeking a world role; the geriatric Western nations, remembering their past glories; the Asiatic states, led again by a resurgent Russia, all sought to impose their will on a world groaning under the twin burdens of its unhappy, underfed billions, and temperatures rapidly depopulating entire regions of the globe.

All circled around each other, looking for weaknesses, looking for an advantage, looking for a method of ensuring it was their world-view that would triumph. Each bloc played out a planetary realpolitik game of Go: unafraid to use violence and terror where that would work for a short-term advantage, but drawing back if the threat of mass annihilation seemed about to materialise. For weapons of death had continued their development into new and more certain methods of murder: it was now certain that the only Archaea and Bacteria would survive World War Three. More complex, more vulnerable, forms of life would be swept away, for the new weapons could unwind the very fabric of matter itself, and disperse it as mist. A rational species, more deserving of survival, would have realised that the dangers were too great and abandoned its insane playing with atomic fire—but such was not the way of humanity. The Late Twentieth century's dreams of mutual assistance through supranational political systems had all been tested in the crucible of reality, failed, and swept aside. Now only endless mutual suspicion and simmering hatreds remained to drive an unhappy world groaning under its burden of human flesh: spiralling to the edge of mass suicide, pulling back for a few moments of hope, only to spiral in again. In this unstable situation, where today's influential victor was tomorrow's pathetic loser, many non-state organisations arose to harvest power and wealth out of misery. Basically non-political, they sold their services to the highest bidder on a purely temporary basis. Usually their employers had two main aims: to control the entire Pacific basin, and to plunder Africa and South America for their natural resources. Which major bloc was selected for destabilisation depended entirely on which other major bloc was doing the hiring at that moment. One of the more violent, and hence more successful, of these groups was known as "The Great Ones". It was their local head whom Gonzales had been sent to eliminate.

Thus, a game of gambling with disaster had evolved: each group seeing how far the others could be pushed. A gamble to ensure the great conflagration did not break out.

A clever gamble.

But it was failing.

A0 and C3 reviewed the situation: or rather, A0 reviewed the situation, and C3 was present to supply additional data if needed—which was not very often.

C3 finally said: 'Gonzales should succeed; he's an effective officer.'

A0 corrected that rash comment immediately.

'Gonzales is an adequate agent, but there are better. I estimate his chance of success as no higher than 45%. But it is essential that I determine that Guang is among the casualties. I do not care about any underlings who will be liquidated: Guang is the prime target. It is essential that Guang be given no way back—his termination is essential to weaken the Great Ones. He knows we are closing in on him, hence this elaborate and highly expensive subterfuge. Gonzales' mission is to terminate Guang. He has the weapons, but if they fail, he only needs to be no more than three metres from the target.'

C3 had no rejoinder to that, so they both returned to watching the scenario through Gonzales' own eyes.

Unaware of the discussion about his abilities that had just terminated, Gonzales noted how the group of figures moved quickly on their wavering columns of exhaust gases, all heading for the coast. No doubt they were anxious to get somewhere before satellite or drone cameras detected them. Those events could not be far off, as the detonations would have been noted worldwide.

Gonzales followed them as close as possible; at no time did the group look behind them; their aim was the coast and they had no reason to suspect pursuit.

They stopped on the shore, scanning the horizon.

They did not have long to wait; a silvery dot appeared at the base of the towering cumulonimbus clouds, and rapidly resolved itself into a smallish jet copter heading straight for the beach and the waiting group.

It never arrived.

Gonzales had unclipped a metal cylinder from his back and, placing it against his shoulder, took aim, forcefully compressing a small button near the cylinder's bulbous end. The recoil as a tiny missile blasted out was enough to knock him onto his back, despite his heavy suit, so he was unable to watch the weapon shoot, arrow straight, onto the oncoming machine. He was also unable to witness the craft instantly transform into an expanding cauliflower-shape of black smoke and evil, red-orange, flame. A few burning shards of debris arced into the waves.

The group's way back was gone.

Its shocked members turned as one, but Gonzales' armoury had not been exhausted by the use of the one-shot missile launcher. He unclipped a handgun and ran directly at the still-astounded figures. His weapon fired five times, but his first target, a man distinguished from the others by the girth of his suit, proved to be amazingly agile, disappearing behind a dune just as an armour-piercing bullet pierced the air where he had been. Two others were not so adept, and fell as the bullet intended for them passed easily through armoured suits, and even more easily through flesh and bone, erupting on the other side in a shower of blood. The third figure was hit in the left shoulder, instantly pulverising bone and shredding muscle and tendon, but whoever was in the suit recovered amazingly swiftly, leapt up from the sand where the impact had thrown him, and came at Gonzales with a long knife that had seemed to instantly materialise in his right hand.

Gonzales fired again and missed.

('An unacceptable error,' A0 observed unemotionally.)

The two antagonists crashed together, looking like miniature carnosaurs in their heavy carapaces. They were so weighed down that their conflict looked almost comic as their battle was played out in slow motion, but it was no friendly tussle on those irradiated sands. Gonzales had no knife, but he had two arms; his assailant had a blade as sharp as obsidian, but only one working arm.

That blade slashed through the outer layers of Gonzales' suit again and again as they swayed together on the beach, the first slice penetrating right through to Gonzales' flesh, although it did not cut him. Gonzales knew the island's atmosphere was not yet too heavily contaminated by fallout and that the air rushing in would have no immediate effect. A good decontamination scrub when he got back would be enough.

The thought gave him enough strength to end the clumsy battle. A wrench on the injured arm was enough to distract the attacker sufficiently for him to lose the knife to Gonzales. The latter made no ineffectual slashing moves but instead made a direct thrust with all his strength at the neck of the suit where it met the shoulder. It went straight into flesh, and the attacker fell heavily to the sand.

Gonzales stood over the fallen figure; blood roared in his arteries triumphantly.

He could do anything! Kill anyone! Win any…

And then he felt the gun in his back. And amazingly, a voice came over his supposedly secure communication channel.

'I think you will drop that knife, my friend. After that, take off your helmet and turn and face me.'

The target—the large man! Unharmed and murderous!

('My probability assessment was too high,' was A0's god-like observation, 'I must check my handling of the parameters.')

Gonzales reluctantly obeyed, dropping the helmet at the other's feet. His enemy did not bother to look down—much too obvious a trick. Instead, keeping a respectful distance from his captive, he, in turn, removed his helmet. Both men were instantly aware of the stink of charred vegetation, the hard, unforgiving odour of splintered and shattered rock.

Gonzales saw a large, swarthy face, narrow eyes, slick black hair—Guang, the commander in chief of the local branch of the Great Ones.

'It's the end, Guang, the Great Ones' terrorism is over. Your gamble failed.'

'And what gamble might that be, Gonzales?' Guang's voice was soft and curiously gentle for a man guilty of so many horrors, 'Don't try to hide your surprise—we knew you were in the area.'

Gonzales' mind whirled. Had Australasian intelligence been penetrated? Who was implicated? But, trying to keep the advantage in the arena of intelligence, he countered: 'We knew you had been employed to destroy the fusion reactor and destabilise this entire region, but you'd realised things were getting too hot for you. So you planned to make it look as if your group had bungled the job and blown themselves up. Then, with the heat off, your so-called Great Ones could spend a few quiet months planning new atrocities.'

Guang gave a small smile.

'Don't be childish. One man's "atrocity" is another's successful operation. The world is going to Hell—everyone knows that. So why not make some money while waiting for the inevitable? All those people who died—they were going to die anyway. Did you think they were immortal?'

As Gonzales listened, he felt a strange doubt begin to stir in his mind. Things were wrong somewhere; there were parts of the mission which now seemed cloudy. Guang's method of escape from the murdered island had been clear enough— but where was his own? Try as he might, he couldn't bring the answer to the surface to reassure himself. But he was certain of one thing: he had to get off this lump of rock. It wasn't immediately lethal, but one rain shower would change that, as the fission products began to fall back from the clouds.

He pushed the doubt away: he had a job to finish.

'Whatever you say, you're finished, Guang. You've been too long on this island—by now a million pictures of you are being examined all around the world. I destroyed your only way back.'

Guang shrugged.

'You're right in a small way. I can't lay low as I originally planned, and my employers no doubt will be somewhat upset. They may even cut my bonus. But I'm too good at my job to be severely chastised. And I'm certainly not stuck on this island like a radioactive Ben Gunn. The Great Ones have more than one copter—even your Intelligence Group must know that—and one is heading here right now. I have my way back, but what about yours? Where is your way back?'

'Option 2 will now be initiated,' A0 said as tonelessly as ever.

'No, it's not certain that he's failed!'

C3 looked up, staring at the large black cube that housed A0's remorseless, dispassionate, intelligence.

Several years ago, various nations, in an effort to leap ahead of their rivals, had started involving Artificial Intelligence in their strategic decision-making. Gradually, more and more of the complex decisions had been handed over to the machines, who would be unencumbered by foolish emotionalism, who would not put too much emphasis on the value of human lives.

Eventually, the AI brains had been given total control of the planetary game of Go, as political leaders came to rely on their vast ability to think hundreds of thousands of moves ahead; to out-think wet animal brains.

Unfortunately, every other player had the same idea.

Having handed control to AI, the humans discovered they could not get it back.

C3 made one more attempt to save her lover's life.

'It's not over yet—he'll think of something!'

'The decision is made,' was the toneless reply.

C3 buried her wet face in her hands.

Gonzales stood two metres from Guang, his mind whirling. This must be the end.
What could he do? How could he distract this supremely confident, efficient killer?

He could not know that intelligent machines had weighed the probabilities from a vast sheaf of possible actions. The machines knew that Gonzales was a good agent. He would get to Guang—there was a high probability of that. He would be brave and resourceful—for that, the probabilities were close to unity.

But his quarry was supremely important. Many of the most recent setbacks suffered by Australasia could be laid at his door.
A0's analysis was flawless.

No, Gonzales could not be fully trusted. He might be too slow, too cautious, miss a chance, suddenly think of C3 and lose focus through sentimentality—no, the risk was too great to leave success to him alone.

Guang must die—and die today, not in a week or a year's time.

Gonzales' suit was heavy for various reasons—most of them to do with shielding from fission reactions.

But one reason was to do with the high explosives woven into the very polymers of the suit's fabrics. Explosive polymers powerful enough to kill a man in an armoured suit as long as he was within a radius of three metres.

And so A0 sent the command.

Instantly on receipt of that command, Gonzales and Guang were both replaced by an ever-expanding sphere of fiery annihilation that gouged a crater in the sand and shattered the carbonised remnants of nearby vegetation into whirling dust. Gonzales should have known.

There was no way back.

PER ARDUA

'Mars isn't a world,' smiled the rotund Professor Charles Rickman, rather condescendingly, it must be admitted. The two of them sat alone, and through the fused quartz window the grey, monotonous lunar landscape could be seen reaching out to a black, starless sky above the close horizon.

Gerda Weber crinkled her white, hitherto unlined brow and, following Rickman's eyes, tugged her skirt toward her knees. She had the slim, long-boned look of someone who had grown up under feeble Martian gravity.

'There you are wrong, Professor. Mars is not populated by worthless parasites like Earth. People who need machines to wipe their bottoms or fuck their lovers for them. We have no novelists, poets, singers, actors—or criminals, for that matter. You may not be aware we have reintroduced the death penalty. No, we are peopled by the cream, the intelligentsia of courage, the steely elite, the scientific flower of Earth's decaying culture. We do not live on a soft world where one can walk in a nature reserve smelling flowers and declaiming how absolutely darling it all is. No, our world is a harsh taskmaster who does not suffer fools gladly, and where one moment's loss of attention can mean a painful death. We fought it from the moment we arrived, and we are conquering it, slowly but surely. We colonists will become the fire-tempered masters of Mars—and then, who knows what else we will master?'

Rickman smiled, a little wryly.

'Quite a speech, my dear girl. It must have taken quite a while to learn it, and perhaps you even believe some of it. It all sounds a bit childish to an old stager like me—all this rugged individualism; the Wild West on another world. I bet you wish there'd been native Martians when you arrived—so you could have herded them into reservations. Or exterminated them, more likely.'

Gerda's lips compressed themselves into a thin line.

'Do not try to insult us, Professor. We have no need of the approval or disapproval of your people. Your opinions are of no interest and no value. However, Mars needs you in the planning of the Stellaria's great adventure.'

Rickman looked suddenly alert.

'The Stellaria. Project Cheiron—the abandoned journey to Alpha Centauri. I didn't think I'd hear that name again.'

Gerda smiled archly.

'Interested, Professor? The gutless Federation of Earth dropped the project, of course; it prefers to waste googols trying to achieve physical immortality, attain flawless beauty, write the most touching love poetry, and other such fantasies. But we know that if Martian culture is to survive, to live, to breathe, to reach its full flowering, we must escape Earth's corrupting influences. Some of our less intelligent people are still at risk of being infected by the decadence of your planet. But our leaders know that Earth is finished. Like Classical Greece, it gave a more warlike culture its original impetus, but now it is withering; its inhabitants inconsolable if they stub a toe. It will not drag us down into its eventual ruin.'

'Mars cannot explore beyond the Solar system.' Rickman felt a growing need to puncture these dreams of lebensraum. 'Its entire population of professional victims is less than that of Paris. Moreover, the Centaurian planets are not fully understood as regards habitability. They may well be just lumps of rock—even worse than Mars.'

Gerda's stare became positively lethal at those remarks, but Rickman continued: 'And a space vessel capable of only 40% of lightspeed is useless for interstellar travel; I hope you understand that's the peak velocity, which doesn't take into account deceleration at the destination. Why do you think Cheiron was dropped—do you think the FoE is staffed by idiots?'

'We already know,' Gerda continued imperturbably, 'that there are many icy bodies between Sol and Alpha. These we can use for replenishing our supplies and reaction mass. And the ship will not be occupied by Terrestrial crybabies whimpering for their mothers, but by Martians. We are used to danger and struggle and risk. In fact, we need it. Just like you need your fine wines and your soft beds. And your pain relief,' she added, her full lips twisting into a sneer.

'Risk or not, you can't do it. The Stellaria was commissioned by a previous administration. And now that we're stuck with it, we'll have to find some use for it. Probably making it fully automatic, so no lives are put at risk, and use it to explore the Oort Cloud. Or something. I don't really care as long as I'm not on it. I get travel sick.'

He glanced at Gerda but, as expected, she had not shown any appreciation of his little joke. Rather wearily, he continued: 'But you people can't use the damn ship in any case. Without an advanced subatomic specialist—which we know Mars doesn't have—you could not control the spiked fusion drive. Without that burning merrily away, you'd have a better chance of getting to Alpha on a push bike.'

Gerda smiled, her scarlet lips suddenly revealing flawless teeth.

'You're right. We didn't have that essential subatomic specialist to whom you referred. But now we do.'

She suddenly looked over her companion's shoulder.

Rickman felt a pad slapped over his mouth, and darkness took him eagerly.

***

The Sun is small in the skies of Mars; a white disk only two-thirds the diameter of the friendly orb of Terrestrial summers. It burns in a strange, pinkish dome, in which, on rare clear days, the brightest stars can be seen through the airborne dust. It is an austere world of limonite sand and basaltic rocks; where the harsh winds blow the sands into barchan dunes, and only dust storms move.

At least, that was how things stood when the first colonists arrived in the twenty-second century. They found a lifeless world with so meagre an atmosphere that water poured onto the ground would explode into vapour and be lost to the frigid winds. A world of desiccated ochre deserts. A world on which the sunshine was far from friendly, but instead laced with carcinogenic radiations.

But they survived.

Slowly, slowly, they grew in numbers; spreading out over the ochre surface. They had great plans, great dreams of how to mould their new home closer to their needs. First, they would give it a magnetosphere so that the relentless solar wind could no longer strip away the precious air. That was Phase One: already complete. Soon they would move on to Phase Two: to build up the atmosphere until water could pool on the surface for the first time in millions of years. And after that would be Phase Three…

But they knew Mars could never be like Earth. It would always be a wild beast, kept chained but untamed; watching, waiting, for its chance to strike at its jailer; to punish these overweening invaders; to remind them that one simple misstep meant sudden death.

The Martians knew this. They knew they must always be ready to face the unchained beast.

And that was the way they wanted it.

And they felt a growing contempt for their distant siblings, who could not understand that life is only meaningful when in the peril of death, that there are worse things than an unkind word or a dead puppy. And that to want a long, calm, hedonistic life is the desire of a child.

And yet those spoiled infants somehow had the effrontery to claim jurisdiction over them!

Berezovsky, a tall, deeply lined man, blackened by Martian UV and whose smile, on the rare occasions that he showed it, was deeply frightening, pointed to a parabola displayed on a monitor.

'Our agents took over the Stellaria from its orbit around Luna, and it is now following this path out of the ecliptic to a distance of 35AU where it will assume a basically circular orbit. It is then absolutely undetectable.'

Dowsett, a small man with a plumpness unusual on Mars, glanced at the monitor. Almost instantly, he absorbed all the implications of the displayed data.

Despite his plumpness, he was a true Martian.

'Fairly undetectable, I'd say. But no matter. Is the physicist under control?'

Berezovsky gave a brief nod.

'Of course. He was taken from Imbriumport and placed on the Stellaria as planned. At present,' Berezovsky turned back to the monitor and jabbed a finger at one end of the arc, 'he's right here—within transfer distance for me to join him on the Stellaria.'

***

Rickman awoke to stars and silence. His head felt fuzzy, and his knees weak. He slowly pulled himself into a sitting position and took in what was obviously a spaceship cabin. A porthole cover slid back under his questing fingers, and he faced velvet night, icy stars and a tiny, pea-sized sun. Either he'd been out for weeks, or he was on a very fast ship. Somehow he preferred the latter alternative. Instantly as that thought ended, there was the sound of a door sliding open, and he turned in time to see Gerda enter. A rather more functional Gerda. Gone was the blouse that had wrapped itself around firm breasts, gone was the skirt that had revealed hectares of nyloned thigh: instead, she was wearing a dark blue overall, rather like a boiler suit. She stood revealed as what she assuredly had always been: a hard, effective agent, and one, as Rickman reminded himself, who was no longer attempting to get the approval of ageing physicists. She reminded him of a sleek panther, patiently waiting for an impala to come into striking distance.

'Quite recovered, Professor?' she queried, giving him another flawless smile. That at least was unaltered.

Rickman, realising that he no longer needed to play the gentleman, gave Gerda a few instructions on what she could do next; some involving quite unlikely sexual activities. Gerda was completely unaffected: obviously, she'd heard a lot worse.

'What the hell do you think you're doing?' Rickman finally spluttered when he'd finally finished giving Gerda his impractical advice on unusual calisthenics.

She was as unperturbed as usual.

'Why abducting you, Professor? What else would we be doing?'

'And for what purpose?'

She took out a thin, gold drugarette and activated it, never taking her eyes off the indignant scientist.

'Why to aid in the fulfilment of the Stellaria's great adventure, just as I told you in Imbriumport.'

Rickman laughed.

'You're insane like the rest of you inbred colonists! Do you think I have any desire to aid your gang of psychopaths and then end my days, having reached a pitiful few percent of the way out to Alpha?'

Pinkish smoke trickled out of Gerda's nostrils. Her pupils had enlarged under the narcotic kick, but she was obviously still completely in control of her faculties.

'Desire has nothing to do with it. You have a son who is at present enjoying his honeymoon in Tahiti, have you not? We can give you the hotel he is staying at, the name of his new partner and the number of their flight home. If you wish them to live, you will also wish to co-operate.'

Rickman's eyes narrowed.

'You people are totally insane. Do you think this is Europe in 1940?'

Gerda shook her head, the bell of raven hair swaying slightly.

'By no means, but you must admit that their methods were very efficient. Violence has always been a most effective method of getting what one wants. And you Terrestrials—you're not very good at dealing with violence, are you? You weep over a split fingernail. Your people say Martians do not have a sense of humour, and they're right. We are not joking, Professor.'

'You bitch,' Rickman said slowly, feeling every syllable in his mouth as he spat them out, 'you filthy, filthy bitch.'

Gerda's gaze was unabashed.

'You won't frighten us with words, Professor. I'm not one of your soft Earth-dolls. On Mars, we deal with far worse problems than words. Don't you have a saying about "sticks and stones"? Mars has made us hard, and we are glad of it. And what we want—we take!'

'And you need the Stellaria? To establish new versions of Mars throughout the Milky Way? My girl, you'll find the stars are not enough. You need people, people with some sense of decency, not self-alienated wolverines who revel in playing the victim. Earth has done you no harm. We seek to maintain some control over you only because we know that your hold on your planet is still fragile. You are trying to expand too fast and paying the price in human lives. Think of your children, who you seem to regard as disposable. Earth seeks to give you a safety net as a concerned parent, not rule you like some sadistic emperor.'

Gerda sneered: 'You've never had to bargain with a Terrestrial agent over the supply of antiradiation drugs, have you, Professor? Deal with babyish regulations about what you mustn't do in case you spill your drink on the carpet! Or be told that your people's population is growing too fast— and that you must stop fucking!'

Suddenly Gerda's drugarette was flicked from her fingers. Instantly Rickman realised from its trajectory to the floor that he had a sense of weight. This vessel was under powered flight.

'Professor, you're so naive. And I, a poor chit of a girl, can understand and you cannot. Of course, we know that the stars are not enough. As of now, we don't want them. Their day will assuredly come, when we are ready. But now we want the Solar system—but without a pre-eminent Earth in it! With Mars as its natural leader, its head! Only we can stop Homo sapiens degenerating into some kind of contemptible sea-squirt.'

'Then then why do you want the Stellaria?'

Gerda's gaze was as cold as a Plutonian nitrogen glacier.

'Any structure containing as much energy as an antimatter-fuelled spaceship is a weapon such as humanity has never before built. Imagine the Stellaria, travelling at a significant fraction of lightspeed, arrowing down from the celestial north pole. We don't need explosives—any kilogram-sized object ejected from the ship as it makes a hyperbolic pass of Earth would impact with such kinetic energy that it would make the dinosaur-killer look like the fall of a feather. There'd be survivors, but they'd never be able to try to boss us around ever again. You see, we would still have the Stellaria, and could return whenever we wanted.'

'You're insane. They'd know it was you maniacs piloting the Stellaria. And flatten Mars.'

'Wrong again. Do you know how long it takes to make a decision on Earth, with all your checks and balances, and hatred of any action that could be interpreted as aggressive? How the thought of any kind of violence makes you wet yourselves? How they will fuss and fumble and blame each other, before they bow to the inevitable and accept our overlordship, in return for no more horrible cataclysms. After all, there is only one Stellaria, and we have it.

'But that's not the real reason for your race's impotence—do you realise just how fast 0.4c is? Nothing like it will have ever been seen in the system before. A few people on the impacted hemisphere will see a blinding trail in the sky, but it is unlikely that their nervous systems will be able to process anything before the relativistic impactor strikes. Don't fool yourself, Professor; there are people on your world who see we Martians as throwbacks, as cavemen with spaceships. The whole colonisation was a mistake they say. Look what creatures it has bred! Those who still call themselves men might decide to try to grow a cock and fight us. Perhaps they are already seeking to find some way around their inbred cowardice and attempt to strike us down before we become too powerful, as we assuredly will. But we will strike first!'

This last sentence was almost screamed out. Rickman stared in horror at the woman, his mind trying to come to terms with the enormity of what he had been told. He found he could only speak in a hiss and finally managed to utter: 'You monster! You unbelievable monster!'

'Not me, Professor. If there is a monster it's a man called Berezovsky. You'll be meeting him, but I doubt that you'll like him. Not many people do.'

Rickman was no longer listening. The image of a smoking crater big enough to reach down to Earth's mantle filled his mind. Then, like an automaton, he leapt from his couch and propelled himself at Gerda, fingers crooked into talons, aiming for her soft throat.

She shot him with a nerve dart an instant after he had started to move and once again, he was enveloped in darkness.

***

Rickman's second awakening was to the humming of a colossal engine, an engine holding even more colossal energies. He knew it was the spiked fusion drive in its calm idling state. Deep within it was a hemisphere of U^{235}, embedded in a blanket of deuterium and tritium. On activation, a beam of antiprotons and positrons would be injected.

And then…

And then … what words are adequate? The conflagration created would be unlike anything ever seen in the Solar system before, a lance of energy so powerful, so potent, so insanely violent, that it would burn bright enough to cast shadows on the surface of the Sun.

No habitable world could be anywhere near that exhaust beam and remain habitable. The full power of the beam would blast away an atmosphere and soften a planetary crust.

But nothing less could propel a material object into the inconceivable speeds that the Stellaria had been designed to reach in humanity's grandest plan—the race's ultimate dream of reaching the stars.

And now, like most things fashioned by humans, it would be a weapon.

His flickering eyelids finally lifted and before him was a vast cliff of metal, so polished that he could see the reflections of his captors before he turned and saw them in person.

Gerda was there. So was a tall bullet-headed man with UV-blackened skin against which a cheek scar showed strangely white.

'Awake at last, Rickman,' he said, in a voice so deep it sounded like boulders rubbing together, 'you took your time.'

'The alarm clock didn't ring,' Rickman snarled.

For this witticism, he received a stinging slap to the face.

'Like all Martians, I have no sense of humour,' the dark man explained, apparently entirely seriously. 'Do you know where you are?'

'Yes, Section B2 of the Drive Chamber.'

The dark man's eyes narrowed in instant suspicion.

'That's oddly precise for a man who's never been on the Stellaria before.'

'My speciality is subatomics, Mr Whoeveryouare. It's not unexpected that I would know that. After all my equations went into the design of her engines.'

'True, but you are a theoretician. I understood that your visit to Imbriumport was for tourism.'

'So it was, but I read a lot. I'm a quick reader.'

Gerda was looking distinctly puzzled by this odd interchange as if some invisible fencing contest was taking place.

As indeed it was.

The dark man obviously tired of the game, and he turned to look at the vast bulk of the catalysed fission/fusion drive: colloquially known as a spiked fusion drive.

'You are a very uncooperative man, Professor. But let us look on the bright side, for a while. Our missile will hit on the opposite hemisphere to Tahiti, so there is every reason to hope that your son will survive. The tsunami warnings are very good in that area, I believe, so why worry?

'Now to business; this drive is the most complex propulsion system humanity has ever created. To operate it, one must control extremely hazardous flows of antimatter. We do not have the knowledge to do that safely. We could learn of course,' he said, with his trademark grim smile. 'We are not unintelligent apes, whatever you people think. You possess that knowledge, given that the current iteration of the drive is a direct consequence of your work, as you yourself have stated. You will operate it efficiently, or your son will suffer.'

Rickman stared up at this horrific man; seemingly a demon carved from anthracite.

'And what if I sacrifice my son for the sake of all the others who will be incinerated by your missile? One life in exchange for hundreds of thousands.'

The other smiled; almost as warmly as the cragged features would allow.

'Well said. You sounded almost Martian then. But…' and he smiled again, and this time there was not the slightest ghost of warmth, 'we can raise the velocity of the projectile when we eject it. It's a simple issue to increase the impact speed to produce an extinction level event. The extinction of Terrestrials, that is. Don't cry, Professor, your people will not be missed; life will go on without you.'

Rickman lowered his head. His captor could see he was beaten. But when he spoke again, he seemed to have forgotten the other's threats.

'Where are we now?'

'About 23AU from the sun,' Gerda replied, somewhat puzzled.

Rickman nodded, not bothering to look at her. She was obviously no longer a significant figure in this drama. The distance she had given was just about what he expected to hear.

The time was near.

'Very well. I'll need full access to the computers, Mister …ah…'

'Fukov,' the scarred man replied. There was no way of telling if he was serious, but Rickman's lips jerked for an instant.

'And you said you had no sense of humour.'

***

The AI devices were not impressive affairs, as Rickman had foreknown; the real technological advances were in the drive itself. The artificial intelligences were standard models, utilising well understood superconducting circuits able to undertake quantum problem-solving.

Hours passed. They must be near now, Rickman thought.

'We shall want at least 0.38c,' the scarred man had rapped.

'You shall get it,' Rickman had promised faithfully.

More hours went by, although to Rickman they seemed like fleeting instants.

Just as he passed the last of the incredibly abstruse equations into the serried rows of machines that people still called computers (even though they bore as much resemblance to the first machines to carry that title as a motion picture does to a stick drawing) he became aware of three men standing behind him.

'Stand aside,' a now familiar basso profundo voice boomed behind him.

Rickman stood up and turned around; as expected, "Fukov" was there, plus two somewhat wizened individuals he had not seen before.

'As I keep telling you, professor,' the dark man said, 'Martians are not fools. Do you really think we would just take your word for what you have done; do you think the possibility of sabotage had not entered our oh-so-primitive Martian minds? These men are the top mathematicians that Mars has. Show them your instructions!'

Rickman activated the screen and stood aside while the two mathematicians examined the serried rows of code that he had displayed for them.

Once they paused the rolling symbols and demanded that Rickman explain what this expansion meant. Rickman complied, and with a curt nod they returned to the screen.

An hour passed. Eventually, the older of the two turned to the scarred man and said: 'The code is clear, Commander Berezovsky. The spiked fusion drive will engage one hour after the final command is given. There is no trace of any self-destruct or shut-down instruction. It appears that Professor Rickman has done what we asked.'

Berezovsky showed no emotion but merely nodded. 'Thank you. You are dismissed,' was all he said.

But as they turned away, there was a sudden clamour of metallic ululations, rising higher and louder: alarm bells. Stern-faced men looked up from their desks, cold-eyed women stopped their deft handling of computer controls. The clamour grew louder.

Gerda had been smoking another drugarette (it seemed that quaint custom would survive only on Mars, despite the shortage of oxygen) and had been casting amused half-glances at her overweight captive. Now she leapt up as if caught in an act of illicit copulation.

'What in the name of Jesus?' she hissed. Her eyes lost a little of their tension as she caught Berezovsky's gaze. HE would know what to do!

The object of her admiration looked up from yet another monitor. 'Terrestrial ships descending from the celestial pole,' he snapped quickly, biting off the words in suppressed fury, 'somehow they've guessed our move in advance.'

For an instant, he stared wonderingly at Gerda, and Rickman saw her wilt under that ferocious gaze. But, apparently concluding she was innocent, he turned from her and bellowed: 'To hell with it. We'll easily outrun them!'

He turned to his captive.

'Can you advance the ignition, give us the speed?'

Rickman nodded.

'Sure. We will probably be able to outrun them on old-fashioned fission power alone until the main drive kicks in. But the command has already been passed for full spiked fusion power. The coding will not allow any attempt to rescind the command for that drive, as your goons confirmed. I just need to issue just one more instruction.'

Berezovsky's eyes narrowed. Rickman seemed far too compliant. What was his game?

But there was no time for interrogation.

'All right, Rickman. Send the instruction, then get to your cabin and await further orders.'

Like hell—Those "further orders" being a bullet in the brain, thought Rickman as he sent the irreversible command into the electronic guts of the machines.

'Gerda will take you there,' Berezovsky snapped, turning away.

'No need,' Rickman said quickly, 'I can find my own way, and I find Gerda's company somewhat distasteful.'

Berezovsky turned back to face him.

'Understood. It's always a little disheartening to find that a woman has no more sexual interest in you than she would a slug, but you must be used to that. I personally find Gerda a most interesting companion.'

Rickman stepped down from the computer dais and, feeling Gerda's perpetually amused and Berezovsky's perpetually suspicious gazes upon him, stepped out into the main corridor. The corridor was almost silent, glistening and cool. But mighty engines throbbed dully within the metal carapace, as deadly streams of positrons and antiprotons were being generated, preparing for their incandescent tryst.

And then he ran! He ran like a man in a nightmare, expecting instant retribution. Not only that, but as it had been some years since he last exerted himself in that fashion; he hadn't foreseen that his thighs would rub together.

He pulled up the mental map of the Stellaria—where were the escape craft?

There!

He leapt into an elevator, went down and across several floors and, as soon as the door opened, hurled himself out.

To be confronted by the back of an armed guard.

Feeling somehow foolish, Rickman crept up on him.

Now how had he been taught to deliver the nerve-deadening blow? Was it like this?

It was, and to Rickman's relieved, and more than a little surprised, gaze the man crumpled satisfactorily to the floor. Spinning around, he pressed a button on the wall, a section of which obligingly slid open revealing a set of cigar shaped objects about twice as long as the average man. He took one step forward—and a pulsed energy bolt passed above his shoulder and chewed a hole in the wall in front of him. Turning, he saw in quick succession two more guards, an amazed-looking Gerda and a ferocious Berezovsky.

'Come here, Rickman,' the latter hissed, 'I think you have some explaining to do.'

Rickman gave no answer but stabbed the interior door control and, as he had been taught, set it to the 'Locked' position. He stood stock still for a moment, amazed at his own resourcefulness. An instant later, the feeling of triumph evaporated somewhat as a pencil-thin beam of incandescent fury began to eat out an elliptical hole in the wall.

Quick now! Success or failure was to be measured in seconds!

He stumbled into the nearest pod, sealed it, powered up and pressed the Eject button.

There was a fearsome thunder, a giant pressure in his back, and the craft leapt forward through the opened escape tube into a sudden blossoming of stars.

And there against the stars, the small, stubby shapes of the Terrestrial vessels, seemingly motionless in infinity.

***

'We've followed them for an hour,' the captain muttered, 'and they're still increasing the distance between us.'

He gestured angrily at the slim, dart shape on the monitor. (At the Stellaria's theoretical top speed, streamlining had again become necessary.)

'We must follow them,' Rickman said soberly. 'We must make sure.'

The captain glanced at Rickman. Was that slight distaste in his glance?

'It's a fearsome fate, Rickman. I wasn't aware that's what you had in mind.'

'Neither was I until recently. But had you not let them slip through your fingers at the Moon, it would not have been necessary. But once they were in control of the Stellaria and out in interplanetary space, the possibility that their monstrous plan would actually happen became too great. Fortunately, our joint employer had allowed for the possibility that they would actually get me on board. The imprinting of the ship's internal structure I'd been given worked well.'

The captain had been stung by the rotund academic's comments. He hadn't expected the little man to be quite so feisty.

'Otherwise, you'd have been scuttling around like a black beetle in a cellar.'

Rickman ignored the somewhat derogatory image: he was tired; deeply tired both physically and mentally. There was a silence.

Eventually, the captain spoke. 'How long?' he said.

Rickman did not look at the officer and seemed to be talking to himself.

'The Martians like to think of themselves as top-rank scientists, but they're not: An environment in which you're constantly at risk of sudden death is no doubt character-building, but it's not the best theatre for research. Why else would they have needed me? No, all the cutting-edge stuff is still done on Earth; despite our weak and feeble personalities. They were ready for me to sabotage the ship—to blow it up in a heroic act, taking those poor xenophobes with me. So they got their top men to check my coding. But they couldn't check it to the point of absolute certainty, otherwise, they could have done the coding themselves. So they were trained to look for commands to cause the drive to detonate—easy enough with antimatter involved. There were none. They looked for commands to render the drive inoperative. There were none. So they stopped and declared the coding safe. But buried in a bit of housekeeping a bit further down were two deadly commands: one made the ship turn, so it pointed diametrically away from the inner Solar system. The other was the opposite of the one they were looking for: a command to turn the drive on—and make it impossible to turn off. They know the ship is heading out of the system, and no doubt by now, they have discovered they can't turn around.

'But the real blow is just about to happen. The antimatter drive will fire any moment now—and keep on firing. In three hours, the Stellaria will be the first manned vessel to leave the inner Solar system.'

'And keep on going,' the captain added sombrely. 'But they're not fools, and they'll be fighting for their lives. What if they find out how to control the drive?'

Rickman's face was as cold and still as marble.

'They may be able to do that. But not in weeks. Not in months. If and when they do, their forward momentum will be so great that throwing the ship into a return arc would take centuries. They won't be coming back.'

As he said that, a terrible guilt stabbed through his being. He saw Gerda, so self-assured with her goddess-like features, so certain of the rightness of her cause; Berezovsky: a leader of men; no doubt possessed of immense courage and ability. What right did he have to condemn them to first despair, and then death, in the blackness of interstellar space?

He finally turned to the captain.

'Perhaps the Martians are right—right when they say we've lost the courage to be no more than languid aesthetes, living our lives as pleasure-seeking polyps, lacking the backbone to actually do things. We're becoming like those sinners in the Old Testament who God made to be afraid of the falling of a leaf.'

'I didn't know you were religious.'

'I'm not,' Rickman replied, 'but there is something wrong with us. Do you know there's a growing movement to abolish space travel because people might get hurt? Not killed, you understand—just hurt.'

The captain obviously found the topic unwelcome. He shifted the subject slightly.

'You took a great personal risk. That's doing something. Your son…'

Rickman smiled tiredly. He would have to lie down soon.

'Not so. Interplanetary communication is still abysmal. The Martians had no actual hold on me. My son was off-world the day before I was. His girlfriend changed her mind at the last moment.'

The captain suddenly stood rigid with amazement.

'There she goes!' he said, pointing at the monitor.

From the Stellaria's stern, there erupted a sudden cylinder of intense blue-violet light, looking like a supernatural searchlight slicing across the stars. The monitor automatically stepped down the brightness of its display so the beam's intensity did not dazzle the merely human eyes watching it in awe. But even when viewed from the safest possible angle, that relativistic exhaust was still awesome, easily able to ionise the thin scraps of hydrogen out here in the Edgeworth-Kuiper Belt into glowing splendour. The ship showed no obvious forward leap; it takes time to accelerate to 0.4c, but its puzzled, alarmed and yes, eventually frightened, crew were shaking off the dust of Sol.

'They're not ejecting,' the captain murmured.

Rickman shook his head.

'They won't. They're too proud, too brave. They'll try to figure it out until it's too late.'

'Perhaps they'll found a colony out there.'

Rickman was getting weary of his endless negatives.

'No, their course was designed purely for the fastest exit from our system; otherwise, it's completely random. I had no time to choose a kinder path for them—so much suspicion. In all probability, they won't pass close to a star for thousands of years.'

'Pity in a way,' the captain said, 'they're a brave, determined lot. It would be good to have them on our side.'

Rickman's inner agony deepened. Why did it have to be this way? Was it a horrible trap that Homo sapiens had gotten into; must it choose to be either pacific, harmless and pleasure-loving, doomed to try to avoid any danger—and eventually even any hint of unpleasantness—so people became afraid even of a harsh word; or to be brave, resourceful, heedless of personal suffering, but also cold, xenophobic and ruthless like the Martians? Was there no way to combine the best of those two worlds?

The captain turned from the monitor and looked straight into Rickman's eyes for the first time.

'You know, when the report of what we have done gets back to the others, whatever the Martians feel for us now will be like the warm hand of friendship compared to what they will feel then. Your name will become the vilest of curses. This incident was the work of a small band of fanatics. But these people,' he gestured helplessly at the monitor, 'will become instant folk heroes, glorious martyrs. And maybe they are.'

Rickman said nothing.

The captain seemed determined to get a response.

'You know Mars will rise in revolt one day—and soon.'

Rickman's eyes were bitter. 'I know,' he replied a little shakily, and his words were a tired exhalation. 'I told Gerda that the stars were not enough, but I look at all this madness, and I wonder—sometimes I wonder whether humankind itself is enough.'

Neither wished to continue the dialogue. As one, they turned back to the monitor.

Like a blazing brand brandished in hate, the Stellaria's blinding trail poured on, tracing a scar of dying plasma against the indifferent stars.

IT'S A LIVING

Charles Green had hit the wall known to all writers as "Writer's Block." Nothing, it would appear, could make the fabled creative juices flow. Indeed, he seemed stricken by a strange lethargy that none of his usual pleasures could shake off; he had gone down to his basement gym and done some weightlifting, used his precious revolver for some target practice, and both had produced—zilch. (He frowned briefly as once again his subconscious reminded him that he really ought to get a permit for that weapon—well, he'd get around to it, one day!)

He looked at the meagre amount of text he'd managed to type that day for Chapter Three of "Strangers From The Stars" and shook his head.

'Old hat,' he grunted and sat back in the chair. The trouble was that science fiction was moribund as a literary genre; hardly any sold these days, now that the reading public no longer trusted science. (It hardly mattered that there wasn't any actual science in "science fiction"—people thought there was, and that was enough). So what was left, now the internet had killed "erotic fiction"? Elves and Wizards and Magic Swords? No, that market was saturated. Women's magazines? No, no, that was the final humiliation; he would never go there.

Thinking deeply, he reached out for his single malt and sipped it absently. He'd have to come up with something soon; he wasn't a rich man and the mortgage wasn't getting any cheaper. Neither was single malt.

Nothing would come: nothing. Nowhere in the dark vault of his mind was that small, flickering candle of inspiration. The few lines of leaden prose he'd managed laboriously to type looked very much as if they would be the final items in the meagre "Collected Works of Charles Green" that the British Library would one day have the honour of holding.

Stretching a little, he stood up and crossed to the open window for a draught of fresh night air. Maybe that would light that bloody subconscious candle! Drawing back the curtains, he looked out upon the dark wastes of the Yorkshire moors; wild and harsh, with thin grass rippling in a cold wind. A silver beacon blazed one degree above the horizon, apparently following the sun into darkness. The sight somehow increased his malaise. Venus! The setting for so many Golden Age SF epics. Take Carson of Venus by Edgar Rice Burroughs, with all its strange monsters and voluptuous Venusian maidens longing for an Earthman to teach them about love. And what was it in reality? A dreadful, lifeless wasteland of rocks, so hot they glowed with their own energies; not a bare-breasted maiden in sight. No, perhaps it would have to be Women's Magazines, after all.

He shivered suddenly in the cold breath seeping through the window and hurriedly closed it, drawing the curtains back some seconds later. Returning to the computer, he placed his fingers on the keys and typed a few more lines in a desultory manner until the feeling of utter boredom swept back over him. He stopped again and looked at what he had written.

No damn good at all, it's just …What was THAT?

THAT was a blaze of intense blue-white light that had suddenly erupted outside the house, flaring through the flimsy curtains and illuminating every object in the room with a cruel glare. It was completely soundless and lasted about two seconds. Then there was only the light of the room again, dim and yellow by contrast with that coruscant splendour.

A hundred explanations jostled for prominence in Green's astounded mind: WWIII: a nearby plane crash; the fall of a meteorite just outside the house; the explosion of an atomic pile somewhere…

He pulled his revolver from the drawer, hurriedly fitted it into his side trouser pocket, and stealthily crossed to the front door.

He jerked it open and yelled into the night air: 'Who's there?'

There was no reply, only the dark wind moodily whistling over the tussocks of grass.

He stepped outside, using the rectangle of light cast by the house to serve as illumination. Ten minutes sufficed to prove that there was no meteorite or missile crater anywhere near, and then, relieved but still deeply puzzled, he returned inside. He stopped dead on the doorstep. There was a THING by his table, supping his single malt.

'Come in,' said the THING.

He went in.

***

'So, you're a being from the stars?' queried Green, trying hard not to wince as he looked at his visitor. After all, three eyes and translucent cilia twitching around a cavernous mouth take some getting used to.

'Yes,' replied the visitor, 'although of course, to me, you're a being from the stars.'

'Yes, yes, indeed,' muttered Green, anxious to get on to more important things; after all, this nice philosophical point had been done to death in hundreds of stories, most of them written long before Green had been born. 'Which star?' he continued, 'Sirius, Vega, Canopus?'

'Oh, you wouldn't know it,' the visitor replied, 'you can't see it from here; it's only a G-type dwarf like your sun.'

Green waited for the weird being to pour itself another slug of his fast-disappearing scotch—which the creature had insisted on mixing with strong cocoa powder—and then he asked, rather feverishly: 'Where's your spaceship? I didn't see it outside. Is it invisible?'

A cilium contracted in bafflement and then extended again.

'Oh, you mean my mode of transport! Well, I didn't use one, of course; such things have been obsolete in my culture for two thousand years. But in any case, you can't use them for long-distance flight; it's all due to the lightspeed barrier. You know about that, surely? No, I came on what you'd call a psi wave.'

'Would I?' murmured Green, remembering that his last book had poured Helium II on the whole subject of psi phenomena.

'By the way,' broke in the creature, 'do you have any more of this excellent liquid? And this wonderful brown compound reminds me very much of a certain drug now banned on my world.'

Green cast an annoyed glance at the now empty Scotch bottle and shook his head, and then, realising that perhaps gestures meant nothing to the stranger, grunted: 'You've drunk it all.'

The being looked crestfallen; which was only natural as his colourful crest HAD fallen.

'Well, never mind. Got any more questions? I adore answering questions.'

'Yes: How do you speak English?'

'I've been studying your race for some time. I checked on the dialect used in this time-period, and I extracted it telepathically from your brain. It has a very simple structure—both the language and your brain, I mean.'

'Could I use your psi wave?'

'No. The energies generated would kill you.'
Pity: he had rather fancied being the first man to go on a guided tour of the galaxy. If that didn't make him a millionaire celebrity author, nothing would. Oh well.

'How long do you live? Your lifespan, I mean.'

The being made a rippling motion (a shrug?) with two of its multi-jointed arms, sending the empty bottle flying.

'Well, technically, I haven't been decanted from the birthing cell yet, for our culture lies about twelve thousand years in your future, but if I had been hatched in this part of spacetime, I'd be about three hundred, with about another thousand to go. We are potentially immortal, of course, but we tire of it all eventually.'

Hmm, he wasn't really surprised. He'd written far more fantastic things in his Galaxy Smashers trilogy.

Hey! That was an idea! He had the chance here to become the most famous writer of SF in the world; before this creature went home, he could give Green a fantastic amount of data on the real universe and its real inhabitants. His writing would be incomparable with others dependent on mere imagination!

'How soon are you going home?' he began eagerly.

'Soon,' was the guarded reply. 'Why?'

'Before you go, I want you to write down all, ALL, you can tell me about the universe outside; you see, I make my living by writing about this sort of thing and …'

'I know all about that,' the creature replied, swivelling two of its eyes back from an examination of Green's "Naughty Nudes of the World" calendar to focus on the writer again. 'I got it from your thought-stream.'

'Well, how about it?'

'Certainly not,' it replied, 'when I said "soon", I was speaking in my terms, not yours. By your reckoning, I'm not leaving for four hundred years.'

'Four hun…'

'But of course. I came here for serious scientific study. You see, your race is extinct in my time, and I've taken a compassionate interest in your species. It is typical of many that have enough intelligence to create existential problems but not enough intelligence to solve them. In your case, amazingly enough, you have degraded your environment to such an extent that it can no longer support megafauna, such as yourself. It is a most unpleasant end for your race—I've only been able to watch it once. Violence is such an alien concept to us that we automatically shut it out of our minds. So to remove all those horrible scenes from the time-stream, I've come here to save you from that most disturbing extinction you have arranged for yourselves. I'm going to save you by giving you things that you had either insufficient time, or insufficient intelligence, to develop. I'm going to accelerate your development by giving you star travel (slower than light, of course), immortality, psi powers, mathematical eugenics, meson power, and many others that you haven't even got names for.'

'WHAT!' screeched Green.

'Why are you so upset? Your thought-stream…'

'To hell with my thought-stream!' Green snapped.

Many thoughts were tumbling through his mind. He knew that when a field of human endeavour becomes familiar and quotidian, its value as drama sinks to zero; viz. the "Lost Civilisations of Africa"; exploring the Amazon; journeys to the North Pole; air travel; etc., etc...

He felt sick.

'Tell me,' he said, in as calm a voice as possible, 'do you have any crime on your world?'

'Crime? Crime? Is that to do with violence? I'll have to look it up…'

'Never mind,' Green said with a nervous smile. 'That answer is enough.'

He took out his revolver and shot his superintelligent visitor from the stars six times in various parts of the body. His third shot must have hit a vital spot, for the creature suddenly fell backwards, pumping out a green fluid.

He lifted the alien being off the cocoa-stained carpet and began to drag it down to the incinerator in his cellar.

'Sorry, who-ever-you-were,' he muttered, 'but a man has to make a living.'

THE VALLEY OF THE SHADOW

The shadows are deep in Alta. When the summer solstice finally arrives and the Sun burns high in the deep blue Arctic sky, they are a rich ebony, like pools of darkness bubbling up from some subterranean reservoir of the congealed essence of night.

In the ice-bound Norwegian winter, the whole land lies under a blanket of such shadows, thick and heavy and black. The green curtains of the Aurora borealis sway and tremble above the dark mountains but cast no light on the bitter snowfields. Even the full moon does little to drive away the ancient darkness; the darkness that mankind has been afraid of since there were human beings on the Earth. Who in those days knew what lay beyond the circle of light cast by the campfire? Who dared to stand at the mouth of the cave and try to penetrate the ancient gloom? Beyond the light, fierce green eyes looked hungrily inward but dared not approach too close for fear of the blazing flames that only these soft creatures knew how to control. The humans, man, woman and child, knew that only the fires, and the dancing light they cast, protected them from the drooling jaws that lay, waiting, in the night.

None of this was in the mind of Marius Larsen as he went about his business that day. He was a practical man not given to irrational fears, and neither was he worried by an overactive imagination. His job was to drive away darkness but only in a stolid, practical sense. He was an engineer, specialising in solar power and other activities connected by that part of the electromagnetic continuum that, in our innocence, we call the visible spectrum. Larsen was a big man, within touching distance of two metres tall—from above—and with a black beard shot through with wiry red hairs; a beard his Viking ancestors would have been proud of.

He was standing in a narrow valley not far from Alta, staring at the grim ramparts of bare, grey rock that hemmed in the valley on both sides; rock that had been gnawed and splintered by the rending teeth of ice over hundreds of thousands of years.

The valley was home to a small cluster of buildings; a hamlet that was small even by the standards of Arctic Norway. This was not too surprising because the valley was not the most pleasant of places to live, for its walls of bitter rock blocked out the Sun except in high summer, so that for most of the year it lay in complete darkness or, at best, a grey morale-sapping twilight. Not surprisingly, its population had an unusually high incidence of chronic disease, including cancer and neurological conditions. But they were strangely proud of their village and showed little desire to move out of the narrow valley.

Despite their apparent reluctance to move, the Norwegian Government was concerned that a younger generation might find the lure of literally brighter lights farther south might prove too much. With that in mind, one of the jobs assigned to Larsen's organisation was to find ways of stemming the population movement out of the Arctic. It was not a major part of his interests, but as a recipient of a Government grant, he was determined to do what he could.

He turned to his senior researcher, Einar Olsen.

'Mirrors, do you think, Einar?'

Olsen was an older man, thin of body and hair, with spare, drawn features. He thought a lot and smiled little.

'It's the obvious answer and has been done elsewhere, but this village is very linear. It would require a great deal of building work to put mirrors all along the cliff tops. Otherwise, you end up with just a spotlight that the whole population tries to get into.'

Larsen grunted.

'Unfortunately, that's also the cheapest solution. To put up microwave converters would risk frying anyone who stepped into the centre of the beam. We're being paid to keep people here as happy Arctic inhabitants, not to turn them into kebabs.'

Olsen shrugged.

'I'd hardly call them happy. They're the most miserable-looking lot I've seen up here. They all look like they've got tapeworms or something chewing on them.'

'Hardly fair, Einar. They've managed to survive in this cold, dark environment without going mad—which I think is more than I could have done. I think it'll have to be mirrors. I'll add it to my report to Oslo sometime next week. Anyway, back to our real work, I think.'

Olsen muttered something that Larsen didn't quite catch but it sounded quite a bit like "Thank God for that".

They climbed into the 4X4 and drove back to the research facility, which stood not far from the narrow mouth of the shadowed valley. Once again, it was Government policy to site such facilities close to the impoverished populations they were trying to keep viable above the Arctic Circle. However, in this particular aim, they had not been successful, as the village population of trappers, hunters and impoverished farmers had been unable to supply any labour above the most basic. As a result, the research station was populated almost entirely by southern Norwegians, plus others from around the world.

The station had been built to resemble Alta's famous Cathedral of the Northern Lights, and its polished metal sides threw back the Arctic Sun in dazzling highlights, causing the eyes to screw up protectively if one caught more than a passing glimpse of them.

Both men threw off their heavy outerwear and made straight for the central hall of the station, where most of the most advanced pieces of equipment were housed.

The cathedral-like atmosphere of the station was greatly enhanced in its central hall with the high vaulted ceiling, dim lighting and cavernous size.

Larsen flicked a switch and great LEDs flashed into a comforting brilliance; comforting because their spectrum exactly matched the Sun's, and their intensity had been carefully calculated to give the maximum illumination without glare. There, in the exact centre of the great room, stood the massive bulk of the most crucial machine housed in the complex, surrounded by cables as thick as a man's thigh. Lesser machines of the same general type formed a circle around the central one, like acolytes doing the bidding of the Archbishop.

Larsen strode up to it and slapped a huge hand against a shining flank.

'There you are old girl. Missed us?'

Olsen sighed.

'Marius, it's only an argon-fluorine exciplex laser—not your latest conquest in the fleshpots of Bergen.'

'Einar, you have no soul. There's poetry in this machine. It's not an everyday high street machine, spending all day every day drilling holes in the retinas of middle-aged nobodies who want to throw away their glasses. This machine is designed to probe the structure of matter; to catch virtual quantum particles popping into and out of existence and generally playing dice with poor old Einstein's universe. We are privileged to be here on the threshold of who-knows-what discoveries. Why they might even put up a statue of you in Alta— made of ice, of course, just like the hotels!'

'Deep ultraviolet lithography is just like drilling holes in retinas—except the retinas are made of silicon. Otherwise, it's just the same.'

'Einar, I'm going to have to take you on a bender in Bergen if you keep on trying to be miserable. You know as well as I do that lithography is only a side-line for this beauty. It's the quantum level that she's going to probe. And we'll be the ones who'll be riding her when she gets there.'

Olsen shrugged.

'Have it your way. But if we have a quantum effect named after us, I want my name first.'

Larsen's grin split his beard, revealing strong, white teeth.

'The Olsen-Larsen Effect. The ratio of the number of knickers pulled down to the number of beers consumed in the fleshpots!'

Olsen's lips might have twitched once, but he showed no other sign of amusement. Obviously, he was used to the big man's coarse sense of humour.

However, Larsen's interest had switched from the laser to the young female technician who had left the control room, which was buried in one of the vast room's walls, and was striding towards them, occasionally taking a detour when encountering a particularly thick cable.

'Good afternoon, sir,' she said, looking like a China doll beside Larsen's imposing bulk, 'the engineers want to know if you are going ahead with today's experiment, they have to ensure that they can supply the current that you'll be needing.'

Larsen looked annoyed.

'If I wasn't, I would have told them by now. So let's take a look at those figures.'

Nervously, the technician held out a computer pad covered in numbers and formulae.

Larsen swore when his gaze had reached the halfway point of the screen.

'They've done it again. Tell them it's 2π, not 4π. Do they want to blow my bloody head off! Now let's go through the rest of it together.'

He drew the technician to one side, turning his back on Olsen, who knew what was coming next. As Larsen discussed the procedures with the technician, an extremely large hand rested on the girl's hip and began to work its way around to her buttocks. She endured the probing for some minutes, and then, when a single finger of the hand began to make its presence felt, she snatched the pad away and, glaring up at him, snapped: 'Yes, I think I understand it all now, sir!' And with that, she marched back over and around the snaking cables to the control room.

Larsen watched her go in silence for some seconds and then gave a great guffaw and, turning to Olsen, gave him a slap on the shoulder which almost knocked the smaller man over.

'Quite a girl that! I got farther than I expected!'

However, Larsen had erred in thinking that his horseplay had been harmless. The technician burst into the control room, flung the pad down and immediately began typing a letter of complaint about her superior's behaviour. In her anger, she completely forgot the correction that Larsen had demanded to be made. When the engineer asked her if it was OK to proceed, she nodded without really listening, and carried on furiously typing.

Out on the experiment floor, Larsen and Olsen saw red lights flash menacingly all around the room, and the words "WARNING: EXPERIMENT IN PROGRESS" appear on a panel above the control room window. Hurriedly, they slipped on goggles and retired behind a lead screen, the top of which was a darkened panel of lead-infused silica. Larsen had to bend down to see through it; Olsen did not.

There was a deep-throated whirr as the great tube of the laser suddenly came to life and began to rise from the support which held it in its resting state. It swung back and forth slightly as if searching for its target. Then, just as suddenly, it came to an abrupt halt as its quarry was detected.

'Here we go, Einar!' Larsen yelled.

Then the great machine flashed into life. Most of its output was in the far ultraviolet, but there was enough residual blue-violet light to make the beam visible as it annihilated the dust motes that lay between its muzzle and the target: a slab of hafnium-titanium alloy.

Suddenly there was an all-encompassing glow of coronal discharges enveloping the laser and arcs of electricity flashed like angry lightning, reaching up into the lofty roof and jumping from spot to spot, leaving discs of metal glowing red hot where they had struck.

'Shut the power, for Chrissake!' Larsen bellowed into his throat mike as a blazing column of raw electrical death came leaping and hissing across the floor towards them. The technicians must have acted before hearing Larsen's roar, for the power died and the experiment room was plunged into almost complete darkness.

Almost, but not quite complete, for on a far-distant wall, Larsen saw a baleful light begin to flicker.

'What the fuck...' he began but stopped as he became aware that a wordless Olsen was pulling at his arm, trying to turn him in another direction.

He turned, and there hanging in the air was a large globe of crackling blue-yellow energy of some kind; a sphere gently drifting along like a child's party balloon, lazily rotating as it drifted. The air was full of the strong bite of ozone, tearing at their mucous membranes and eyes.

'Ball lightning,' whispered Olsen, 'I've read about it but never seen it. We've created ball lightning!'

'Never mind that!' Larsen roared. 'It's heading straight for the laser! It'll blow millions of dollars' worth of kit sky high!'

Both men stood up as one—but how do you stop a spinning ball of unknown energy?

Without time to think, they picked up the only things near to hand—metal poles—and decided to try and push it away from the laser.

As one, they rushed up to it, and as one, they tried to push away the sphere with the poles.

And as one, they were thrown unconscious to the floor as the ball lightning disappeared with an eye-tearing flash and the sound of a thousand thunders.

***

Larsen felt he was slowly floating to the top of a deep, black subterranean lake that was reluctant to release him. Eventually, he managed to open leaden eyelids and was confronted by the lined face of Doctor Karlsen.

'Ah, you're back, Marius,' the doctor said. 'Good to see you.'

Larsen felt that every movement was like forcing his way through solidifying cement, but by strength of will he pushed himself into a sitting position.

'How long have I been out?' he said, and was disconcerted to hear how weak his voice was.

'Two weeks. You've taken quite a beating.'

'How do you mean?'

'Your general physiology is not too bad—except for one consequence which we'll come on to—but your nervous system took a tremendous jolt. It sent every neuron into a gibbering frenzy—if I can use the technical jargon—but it was the effect on your brain that most worried me.'

'Go on.'

Dr Karlsen seemed lost for words for a moment.

'Well, there were patterns of electrical activity in your brain that I'd never seen before and neither had the textbooks. I feared for a while that you were lost to us. But you had moments of lucidity which gradually became more frequent, so I was reasonably sure you would pull through. And we had the example of Mr Olsen as well, of course.'

'Einar—he's OK?'

Dr Karlsen looked slightly confused, as if unsure of what to say next.

'Well—physically, he seems to have recovered. But you'll meet him later, and you can judge for yourself.'

Larsen frowned at that strangely ambiguous statement but then he shrugged and said: 'It's OK for me to get up now I take it?'

Karlsen nodded.

'Your obs seem fine now. You'll be very weak, of course, after two weeks being bedridden—but there's one consequence of your little accident that you should learn about sooner rather than later.'

He brought a small mirror to the bed and indicated that Larsen should look into it. Larsen did so and was astounded by the face he saw. He was completely hairless—even his eyebrows and eyelashes had disappeared!

'It's permanent, I'm afraid,' Karlsen continued, in a tone which suggested he found the whole situation slightly amusing, 'Every follicle was destroyed. I'm afraid you'll need false eyelashes to protect your eyes.'

Larsen rubbed his chin, finding the sensation of smooth skin extremely odd after many years of a full beard. Then he ran his fingers over the pink expanse of his newly revealed scalp.

'OK, they say it's a sign of virility, don't they?'

Karlsen gave a somewhat crooked smile.

'Well, I didn't think you had any worries there.'

Larsen put the shock of his new appearance behind him: he had work to do.

'I'd like to see Einar now.'

Any trace of a smile vanished completely from Karlsen's lips.

'I'm afraid Mr Olsen's recovery has not been as complete as yours, Marius.'

'In what way?'

'There appears to be…' Karlsen fell silent for some seconds, 'psychological damage.'

'Really? In which case, I must insist that I see him now.'

Karlsen put his hand on Larsen's shoulder.

'Marius—be warned—he's not the Einar you knew.'

'I'll get dressed. Then I'll see Einar.'

Olsen was lying on his back in the cubicle when Larsen went in. His eyes were wide open, and he was staring unblinkingly at the ceiling. Like Larsen, he was completely hairless, but in his case the difference was not as great.

Larsen stood over him, his mass cutting off Olsen's view of the ceiling.

'Einar, Einar! It's me, Marius!'

Olsen made no movement whatsoever. His eyes remained wide open and unblinking.

Larsen leaned down and gently shook his friend and colleague.

'Einar, it's me! What's the matter?'

Olsen slowly moved his head, slowly as if he had to think about every millimetre of movement.

'Marius—is that you? You're alive. You're alive.'

'Yes, I'm alive and ready to kick ass, and so are you, man. It takes more than ten zillion volts to see a tough old dog like you off!'

Olsen's face had not shown any great emotion of joy or relief, but now it changed into a hideous mask of fear.

'Marius—we've got to get out of here! Far away—as far away as possible! Far away, I'm telling you! Don't leave without me—please don't leave me!'

Larsen instinctively straightened up, shaken by this unexpected display of terror.

'Why do we have to leave, Einar? What's wrong, old friend?'

Olsen tried to sit up, but he was too weak and fell back heavily.

'Don't let them turn the lights off, Marius! Leave them on, for God's sake!'

'The lights—why leave the lights on? What difference do they make?'

Olsen began turning his head back and forth as if searching for some hidden danger.

'Shadows,' he muttered, 'shadows. No shadows. There must be no shadows. No shadows I tell you!'

The last was screamed.

Larsen leaned in again. This was worse than he had expected.

'Why no shadows, Einar?'

Spittle formed at the edges of Olsen's cracked lips. Blue veins stood out on his forehead.

'Monsters,' he finally whispered, 'monsters in the shadows.'

Larsen stood up abruptly. Olsen had obviously suffered serious neurological damage in the accident; no doubt due to his greater age. There was no more he could do here; only medical professionals could help Olsen now. He looked down on the frail figure of his friend, now oblivious of his presence and rolling back and forth in the urine-soaked bed.

'Take it easy, Einar. I'll call in again tomorrow.'

As Larsen closed the cubicle door, he cursed the whole research facility and the twist of fate that had ruined his friend's life. And what of his own life? It seemed he had, by blind chance, escaped Olsen's fate, no doubt due to his stronger constitution. He would find some way of dealing with the dramatic change in his appearance, that was a trivial problem compared to Olsen's situation. But his career might well be over. There would be an official inquiry in which every minute detail of how he had run the project would be dragged in the open. Larsen was well aware that there were some women who had objected to his treatment of them; no doubt they would be eager to dig their claws in if they got the chance. And how had that overload happened? Someone had taken a slipshod attitude to safety, and Larsen had an uncomfortable feeling that he was that person.

He returned to his room, ignoring both the curious glances from those who didn't recognise him, and the salutations from the majority who did. Even bald as an egg, it was difficult to mistake him. He sat on the bed for a while, head in hands, thoughts whirling his head like moths around a lamp.

Eventually, he sat up straight. He would deal with these problems in the morning, now he would try to relax. Drink is expensive in Norway, but on Larsen's salary, he could easily afford single malt whisky. He poured himself a large shot, and, moving to his chair, leaned back, glass in hand.

The light in his room was mild and diffuse.

The shadows were faint and ill-formed.

Larsen finished his whisky and put the glass down on the desk.

Then he stiffened.

Had there been a movement within his dim shadow? A kind of sudden ripple?

Of course not. After a day like this and too much whisky, it was a miracle he was still sane.

He fell back on the bed and soon, fully dressed, he was deeply asleep.

***

Larsen surveyed the experiment hall. Nothing had happened since that dreadful day when that weird sphere of unknown force had materialised from the maelstrom of escaped energies that had brought the heart of a massive thunderstorm into the building. There was no smell of ozone or burnt insulation, no charred remnants of fused machines. In fact, very little damage had been done; the whole incident had not lasted more than a few minutes and his and Olsen's mad attempt to save the great laser had been successful. It still sat there, cyclopean and powerful but completely silent. Without Larsen's guiding hand, no one had the authority to turn it on. But as Larsen stood there, he knew some of his authority had gone with his hair. He had been the one who had given the order for the experiment— an order which had nearly destroyed the complex and had driven one man mad. Two weeks had passed since he had seen Olsen and the man was no better. He was still terrified of darkness and still raving about monsters.

He looked at Eriksen, who had taken over from Olsen until the latter was fit to return to duties.

And when will that be? Larsen thought helplessly.

Eriksen did not have the easy familiarity with Larsen that Olsen had had, in fact, there was a slight tinge of mockery in his attitude; the challenge that comes from a subordinate when he sees that the dominant male has been wounded.

'Could you say that again, sir?' he said, even though Larsen was sure he had spoken both loudly and clearly.

'I said,' Larsen said slowly, 'that we'll conduct experiments only with these hand-held lasers until the main machine has been fully tested. Got that?'

'If you say so, sir.'

Larsen might have lost his hair, but he had not lost his bulk. He spun Eriksen around like a child's top and glared down at him.

'If you've got something to say to me, mister, let's hear it.'

The hand-held lasers had a disconcerting resemblance to an automatic pistol and, no doubt unconsciously, Larsen was holding the muzzle against Eriksen's belly.

Eriksen obviously decided that enough was enough for the moment and merely replied meekly: 'No sir.'

'That's more like it,' Larsen growled, 'Now give the ceiling lights a test.'

Eriksen pressed an icon on his computer tablet, and the great LEDs in the ceiling flashed into full power. Larsen and Eriksen studied them carefully, looking for any change in their output caused by the great electrical surge that had swept through the experiment hall.

'They seem OK, sir,' Eriksen observed, 'voltages are right on the button.'

Larsen pointed to one corner of the cavernous room.

'What about that one?'

One of the LEDs was indeed flickering and sending shadows jumping on the floor; their motions somehow suggestive of living things. They walked over until they were directly under it.

'Has to be replaced,' Larsen grunted, ''We've got enough problems without inducing epileptic fits in the staff. See to it, will you.'

He was about to turn and walk away when his peripheral vision caught something. The dancing shadows—what was it that he had seen? Had he seen anything? To Eriksen's obvious puzzlement, he stood stock still, staring at the floor where the shadows were appearing and disappearing. Yes— the central shadow—there was something there. Larsen turned his head slightly so that the dim images would fall on his fovea and squinted slightly.

It was difficult to be certain—the image was grey, faint and fuzzy, like an image of images that have been photocopied over and over. It seemed to come and go on randomly as if taunting him to confirm that it was really there. Eriksen was about to say something, but with a wave of a massive hand Larsen silenced him.

Yes—there; the transient image appeared to be three red dots arranged in a perfect equilateral triangle, right in the centre of the largest leaping shadow. If he moved his head slightly—they disappeared. If he moved his head back—there they were, stable, stationary and unblinking in the centre of the shadow.

'Eriksen, do you see that?'

'See what, sir?'

'Look at that shadow, man. There in the middle of it—do you see three red dots? Like small lights?'

Eriksen looked where Larsen was pointing.

God, he's really starting to go, were his only thoughts, as soon as the investigation gets underway, he's finished. Room at the top for an ambitious guy like me at last!

'Well, sir, the light clearly needs replacing. That constant change in illumination could be quite dangerous. A trip hazard at the very least.'

Larsen clasped the younger man with a grip of iron.

'Stop shitting me, Eriksen!—What do you really see?'

Three red dots? What kind of hallucination is this? At least see a pink elephant, man!

'I don't see anything unusual, sir. Just a possible trip hazard.'

'You don't see anything else?'

'No sir.'

Larsen turned back to the flickering shadows, ready to drag his subordinate like a rag doll across the floor to the strange display.

They were gone.

There were no red dots in the shadows.

'Alright, Eriksen. The rest of the lights seem OK. Get onto replacing that one at once,' he said in a strangely quiet voice.

'Certainly, sir. I'll get a detail up there first thing in the morning.'

Larsen's face was a mask of fury as he stared down at Eriksen.

'Are you hard of hearing, mister? I said NOW!'

And with that, he turned and left the hall leaving behind a subordinate who was baffled and more than a little frightened.

***

Larsen looked at Dr Karlsen.

'So there's nothing unusual about my eyes?'

'Nothing at all. You're slightly long-sighted, but there's no macular degeneration or other nasties. For a man of your age, I'd say your eyes are above average. No need to worry about glasses to go with your …'

He was about to say "baldness" but thought better of it. Larsen was clearly not in the mood for jokes, for his next words were a business-like monotone.

'I take it there're are no changes at all to the lens, the retina…'

'None whatsoever. I've checked the numbers against your last examination, and everything is as it was.'

'But that electrical jolt. It must have had some effect.'

Karlsen gave a friendly, family-doctor-type smile.

'No Marius, this isn't the movies. You haven't developed X-Ray vision, so I'm afraid you can't see through lead, or, in your case, women's outer garments. Nor have you suddenly got telescopic vision. You're just a man. A damn big man but a very healthy damn big man.'

Larsen persisted.

'But what about the brain? You said the electrical patterns in my brain went haywire.'

Karlsen's expression became serious.

'Well, most of vision is actually constructed in the brain; that's well understood now. But the camera part of your visual system—the eye—that's unaltered. You're responding to the same old minute part of the electromagnetic spectrum that you always have done. No extra information is reaching your visual cortex, so you will be no better and no worse than before the accident.'

Larsen finally said what he had hoped to avoid saying.

'What about hallucinations?'

'Visual hallucinations?'

'Obviously.'

Larsen related to the doctor what he had seen.

Karlsen frowned.

'You're not prone to migraines as far as I'm aware.'

'I'm not.'

'Well, as far as we know, you haven't had a migraine up until now. But that doesn't mean that you can't develop them. And visual disturbances are a normal part of migraines—we call them "the aura." Some migraines are stress related—and you've certainly had enough of that recently. Just the shock of losing your hair…'

Larsen looked down at his hands and frowned. It was possible. He had always seen himself as a guy who ate stress for breakfast. But that was ordinary work-related stress, timetables, man-management, deadlines… Not major career-wrecking incidents or the loss of his oldest friend to insanity.

'Is there anything you can do for migraines?'

'Well, regrettably, migraines aren't all that well understood. They're certainly related to electrical activity in the brain so it's quite likely that the jolt you had has caused you to develop them. There are drugs, but they're not terribly effective. And you'd have to give up the whisky.'

'A small price to pay,' grunted Larsen as he rose from the chair in the consulting room. 'When can I start?'

'Straight away. But you shouldn't take them continuously. As soon as you feel the aura coming on, pop the stated number down with a glass of water. Water, mind you!'

Larsen grinned. He was feeling better already. What the Hell had he been worrying over!

'If you say so, doc!'

After leaving the surgery, Larsen went straight to the room where Olsen lay.

'Any change?' he said to the nurse, before drawing back the curtain that hid Olsen from the rest of the room.

'None, I'm sorry,' she said.

Larsen went straight in leaving the nurse looking slightly confused. What had happened to the mild flirtations she had previously had with him?

There was a figure in the bed, curled up in a foetal position.

'Einar, it's me—Marius.'

The figure rolled over slowly, tried to sit up, failed and fell on its back.

'Marius—have you come to take me away?'

'No, Einar—you're not well. You have to stay here until you're better. Then we can go out together and sort that damned valley out—just you and me, like the old days, eh?'

Olsen grabbed Larsen's arm.

'No, you don't understand. They know I can see them. When the lights are turned off, they come out and taunt me. They say horrible things.' His grip on Larsen's arm became like a hoop of steel. 'You said you'd take me away. You promised you'd stop them from turning the lights out. You promised! You promised!'

Larsen did not know what to do. To see his friend reduced to a whimpering beast was more than he could bear. He patted Olsen's bald head.

'Cheer up, old man. The nurses are looking after you. You'll feel better soon.'

With that, he turned abruptly and walked out. As he walked down the corridor, he could hear Olsen calling feebly after him.

On returning to his room, he pulled his laptop towards him and began typing; not without some difficulty due to the size of his fingers.

He searched for everything to do with migraines but particularly the symptoms. As he did so his frown grew deeper and deeper. None of the characteristics of the onset of a migraine were anything like what he had experienced; particularly, there was no mention of three red spots in an equilateral triangle. Automatically his fingers went to his upper lip to tug the moustache that was no longer there; a habit he had when in deep thought. Was Karlsen keeping something from him? Was he deliberately downplaying the seriousness of what had happened to Larsen's brain? He decided to go back to the infirmary.

He strode along the steel corridor, deep in thoughts that were gradually becoming more unpleasant. Suddenly he became aware of a crackling noise, and up ahead was a flashing electric blue glare. For a second, his mind whirled until he remembered that maintenance work was scheduled for this part of the corridor; someone was using an oxy-acetylene torch.

And so it proved. Three men were clustered around the torch which was cutting into the curved metal of the corridor wall. The men had been turned into black silhouettes by the fierce blaze of the torch. And that intense blaze was throwing deep shadows onto the far wall.

And in each shadow were three crimson spots, each one part of a perfect equilateral triangle. For a full minute he stood there, waiting for the illusion to pass. Twice he shook his head; twice he shut his eyes. But no—each time he looked again, they were still there.

And then it happened—as he stared at the shadows, each set of three spots swivelled within the umbras of the shadows—swivelled as if they were aware of him. And in that moment, Larsen knew—knew that they were indeed aware of him, just as Olsen had said that they knew he could see them.

He was interpreting the red spots as eyes.

Larsen was a brave and powerful man; once he had fought off a starving polar bear in Svalbard armed only with a pick axe. But this sight sent a deep electric shock coursing down his spine. His knees buckled, and he found himself leaning against the corridor wall for support.

All his fears had come true. The electric surge he had experienced had destroyed part of his brain—he was now seeing things that were not there. He needed help and fast before the deterioration became irreversible.

At that moment, his throat mike crackled. He moved on past the workmen who were totally unaware of him, momentarily coming between the glare of the torch and the weird shadows it was throwing. He did not look at them.

Once past the noise of the torch, he touched the speak button and rasped: 'Larsen here.'

'Dr Karlsen here. Marius, please come to the infirmary immediately.'

Larsen did so, and Karlsen rose from his seat to meet him as soon as the door opened.

'Marius—it's bad news. Einar…'

Larsen stared at the distressed doctor.

'Speak, man!'

'Marius, come with me. And be prepared for the worst.'

Together they went to the cubicle where Olsen lay and looked down on his corpse; Larsen still hoping that somehow there had been a miracle and that the man who had stood by his side for so many years would be lying there, smiling.

Olsen lay in a strange position: he was half raised from the bed but had not completed the movement nor fallen back. His hands were over his eyes as if trying to shield them or not see something. Below the hands, his mouth could be seen, frozen in a rictus of terror. The body was completely rigid, as if he had been replaced by a shop mannequin.

Larsen turned to the doctor.

'How did he die?'

'We're not sure—it seems to have been a heart attack or stroke.'

Larsen looked down at the doctor with angry eyes.

'You don't know, do you? And how long ago did he die?'

'The nurse says it couldn't have been more than fifteen minutes ago.'

'Fifteen minutes—then how do you explain this?'

Larsen prodded the dead body, which fell heavily to one side as if made of stone.

'Rigor mortis after fifteen minutes. What's going on, Karlsen?'

'Marius —I just don't know. It's unprecedented. It must be something to do with that electric shock. This isn't my field, you know.'

'Look at his face, doctor. That's not pain on it— it's fear. A terrible, all-encompassing fear. How can you be afraid of something that happened weeks ago?'

Karlsen tried to reassert his authority.

'We'll do a post-mortem, of course. I'm sure we'll find that the electrical jolt weakened his heart. It probably threw the rhythms out of kilter in a progressive way, leading to VF. I'm sure that's what we'll find.'

Larsen found that he was losing faith in everyone around him.

'I wonder, doctor. You know, I think you've no more idea than I do about what's going on here. Well, do you?'

'The symptoms are certainly unusual,' Karlsen mumbled, 'I may have to contact my colleagues in Tromsø. I…'

'Yes, do that, doc. Maybe they know how to diagnose a migraine when someone actually has one! Why don't you get a shrunken head out of your bag of tricks and a magic bone and start waving them around? They're more your style!'

Karlsen looked shocked but did not reply.

'I'll be in my room if anyone wants me!' snarled Larsen, 'And I'm not mad. I gave the proper instructions for that laser experiment—I know it!'

He strode angrily down the corridor, unheedingly knocking lesser mortals out of his way without a word. A gnawing fear was rising in him, a fear he tried to push back into his subconscious from whence it was trying to crawl. What if what he had thought he had seen, he had actually seen? Were there things in the shadows, just as Einar had said? He recalled that the apparitions had appeared when there were bright lights and deep shadows. As a scientist, he knew the drill—repeat the experiment under the exact controlled conditions and see if the phenomenon was reproducible. Then Good God— he would reproduce the experiment, and if there was anything hiding in the shadows, he would drag it out by its stinking throat!

He crashed into his room, poured a slug of whisky and called Eriksen.

'Eriksen? Get me the highest wattage solar lamp you can find in this shithole and bring it to my room now!'

Eriksen, who was in the middle of devouring a roll mop herring when he received the unwelcome call, now knew what his boss meant when he yelled "NOW!" and, throwing his meal to one side, ran out of the room. Shortly afterwards, he appeared at Larsen's door, clearly buckling under the weight of the large lamp he was carrying. Larsen tore it out of his hands as if it were made of papier maché and, without a word, slammed the door in Eriksen's face.

He plugged it in and positioned where it would throw the maximum shadow and switched it on. The light exploded like a nuclear detonation; burning so brightly that it obliterated all the fine detail of objects in his room. But it threw a shadow of deepest black on the floor.

'Alright,' Larsen growled, 'if you're there, I'm coming to get you.'

He stared at the shadow.

Nothing.

'Come out and face me, you fucker. Either I'm mad or you're real, and I'm going to stay here until I find out!'

Then it started.

In the centre of the shadow, there developed a strange rippling motion as if a viscous liquid was being agitated from below. Then vaguely glimpsed forms were dimly visible: there seemed to be antennae as thin as human hairs whipping back and forth; then a crawling amoeboid mass fluctuating in size with questing pseudopodia being extended and retracted; then there appeared to be jointed legs flexing and straightening—all in total silence.

Larsen's massive body stiffened. His face went rigid, and electric currents seemed to be coursing down his body.

Einar was right! Perhaps madness was preferable to this!

Finally, in the centre of the writhing mass of unidentifiable structures three deep crimson spots appeared in a perfect equilateral triangle.

'What in the name of all the hells are you!' he hissed.

Just as he said that, the laptop behind him made a strange ululating noise that he had never heard before. Automatically he spun around to look at it. And there, on the screen, appeared the words:
'Hello, Marius. It's good to meet you.'

He snatched the laptop off the desk and turned so that he could see it and the thing in the shadow simultaneously.

'I asked you what you are.'

'A reasonable question in the circumstances,' the laptop typed by itself. 'You are, of course, aware that time is quantised.'

Larsen felt light-headed, as if he could faint at any moment. This experience was gibbering madness—talking to a shadow by means of a laptop computer!

Please let me wake up soon and pour myself some strong, jet-black coffee, a distant part of his mind whimpered.

'Y-yes—I suppose so,' was what he eventually replied. 'What has that got to do with where you come from?'

'I understand your confusion. This must be very strange for you. We come from a nearby continuum in hyperspatial terms. But once here, we exist between the quanta of your timeline or, as we prefer to regard it, you exist between the quanta of our timeline.'

'When did you come here—you things!'

'In a way, we have always been here. As we exist outside of your timeline we can enter at any point and have always done so. We cross to this realm by means of a transdimensional bridge; a structure which cannot be understood by merely organic brains.'

'Why do you hide in the shadows?'

The laptop typed silently: 'Hiding is perhaps an inappropriate word. It is not "hiding"; it is "concealing." Our world would be one of near-darkness, if you could visit it. Which, of course, you cannot. When we first entered this timeline, we found the glare of a G-Type star intolerable. So, initially, we seek shadows and darkness, although any surface which reflected light better than it absorbed it would serve almost as well. And so when we transfer to the surface of your world we seek to emerge in areas of low illumination, and use those as bases to spread out. There is a valley near here which serves as an excellent entry point.'

The shadowed valley Einar and I were going to fix! Larsen thought.

'But,' he continued grimly in his weird cross-examination of a shadow, 'you haven't said why you have come from your world of darkness to ours of light.'

The laptop continued to type words devoid of emotion, of compassion.

'Why it's very simple. We are parasites, and we are parasitic upon you.'

194

Larsen somehow had known this would be the revelation. He closed his eyes, but the terrible blazing light had made his eyelids almost transparent.

'Parasites?'

'Well, that was not very well explained—we are actually parasites upon the fields emanating from nervous systems, and the more complex those systems are, the more nourishment they provide. Those in our lower echelons have to make do with simple lifeforms—molluscs, annelids and so on. Only the uppermost stratum has access to human beings. But as we can access any part of this time stream, we have been directing the development of animal life in the direction of nervous complexity ever since the Cambrian. We are not infallible, of course—the dominance of the dinosaurs, despite their inferior nervous systems, over the mammals that we had been developing, was a complete surprise. But one that worked itself out eventually.'

'Parasites! So you come here to kill us!'

'Of course not! I'm surprised at such sloppy thinking—but you are not a biologist, I suppose. A well-adapted parasite does not kill its host—that would be self-defeating. Which is not to say that our feeding is not without its effects—they manifest themselves as shortened lifespans, the development of degenerative diseases. That is unavoidable.'

That explains those poor people in the valley, Larsen thought, *surrounded by the...'*

'So, what do I call you — before I kill you, that is?'

'We are the *hran*. It simply means "The People", of course.'

'I am going to kill you all.'

'That will be difficult. The accident that allowed you to see us was a freak. No one else can see us. They will lock you up.'

'Einar could see you. And you killed him.'

'And that was unfortunate. Some of the lower-order hran, who had only recently emerged, seemed to take delight in tormenting the poor man. I was not aware of it until it was too late to prevent your friend's sad demise. I do hope they do not similarly visit you whilst you are incarcerated in whatever mental hospital the authorities choose for you.'

'Spare your crocodile tears, parasite. There is only one thing to do with a parasite—cut it out, throw it on the fire and watch it squirm and burn.'

'Mere words, I'm afraid. The threats of a frightened child. You have not grasped what we truly are. We are everywhere in your timeline and always have been. In every land, however dominated by your Sun, there are always shadows. We can exist in bright light in a dormant form and spring to life when a single shadow forms.'

'I will kill every stinking one of you.'

The laptop typed on, unconcerned, uninterested in his threats.

'Everywhere there is darkness, we are there. Your primitive ancestors feared darkness as they huddled around their little fires. They were afraid of the carnivores, of course, but their fear remained even after the beasts had been driven away. Because your ancestors knew we were there; they knew we were outside the ring of light watching them, hungrily waiting. Some of your shamans and witch doctors could see our eyes, without having to pass through your kind of trauma. They knew eyes were watching them beyond the cave, waiting for the night to descend so they could claim their prey and feed.

'And your children, let us discuss them. They know we are there, however much you tell them that there is nothing to fear, because the children know the truth—that there is indeed something to fear in the darkness; something watching them. That's why they beg you not to leave them, beg you to leave the light on.

'And here is some information especially for you, Marius. I am YOUR parasite. You did not compel me to appear—I came because I wanted you to know the truth. Sometimes I emerge from a shadow in the night, and I sit on your chest and look down on you. You know I am there because you toss and turn and make little moaning noises. But in the morning, you just put your feelings of tiredness and sadness down to bad dreams. But it was me.'

'All of you. Dead.'

'Marius, you live in this land of polar night with its impoverished biota, but you may have seen nature documentaries about the vampire bats of South America. Have you seen how in the night, they creep silently along the ground and bite the ankles of the cattle; little bites that the cattle don't feel because of a natural anaesthetic in the bats' saliva? Because of that seeming kindness, the cattle are unaware of the bats as they bite and bite, revelling in the warm, life-giving liquid that they suck from those stupid beasts. The parallel is exact.

'We hran are the vampire bats. You are the cattle.'

Larsen's right hand slowly, slowly moved along the desk to where he had put his hand-held laser. Using his peripheral vision, he could see the setting was in the normal range. A great thumb slowly turned the dial to 200 nanometres—the deadly far ultraviolet.

He began triumphantly to chant: 'Though I walk through the valley of the shadow of death,
I will fear no evil; for thou art with me.
Thy rod and thy staff, they comfort me. '

The hran did not respond: apparently unsure of what Larsen was doing.

Suddenly Larsen roared: 'Try this rod, you bastard!'

And with that, he pointed the laser at the three red eyes and fired the device. Out poured the invisible death of the lethal far ultraviolet radiation, concentrated into a narrow beam of intolerable energy. The hran writhed under that rapier of raving electromagnetic violence. Writhed, twisted—and then suddenly vanished.

The hran was gone.

***

Larsen spent the night almost perpetually awake. Hundreds of plans whirled in his mind.

He knew what to do. First, the ramparts in the shadowed valley must be dynamited, letting the healing sunlight into its depths, freeing its enslaved inhabitants from the jaws of the hran. Next, neuroscientists must examine his brain to discover what had changed, so people could be trained to see the hran without going through Larsen's trauma. Then warriors armed with lasers and powerful solar lamps would hunt the hran down; every shadow in which the parasites lurked would be obliterated in beams of visible light followed by blasts of deadly, invisible radiation onto the squirming creatures that had lain hidden within.

Larsen felt absolutely exhausted even though the day had hardly begun. But he knew what to do.
He walked groggily over to the mirror above the washbasin.

At least he didn't have to waste time trimming his exuberant beard anymore.

He looked in—and stopped.

His reflection was not looking at him.

As Larsen stared, the face in the mirror turned to regard him speechlessly, unemotionally, with eyes that glowed crimson.

The laptop behind him made a strange, ululating noise, and words appeared on the screen.

He rushed over and read the words.

'Hello, Marius. It's good to see you again.'

AFTERWORD

The story of Marius Larsen and the hran continues in the novel "Hideous Night".

After years of increasing despair, Larsen finally meets someone who has the ability to help him in his battle to save humanity from the jaws of the hran.
But can he make her believe his fantastic story?

The novel reaches its cataclysmic climax in the hideous night of the oppressor's own world.

ACKNOWLEDGEMENT

Once again, I must thank Terry Evans – thanks for all the covers!
His website may be found at:

www.terry-evans.com

ABOUT THE AUTHOR

Martyn Rhys Vaughan was born in the World Heritage steel town of Blaenavon which nestles among the green hills of the south Wales valleys.
From a very early age he was interested in how the Universe works and what it contains. He listened to early space travel adventures on the radio, such as Journey Into Space and devoured the few American magazines of unusual and unlikely adventures which happened to come his way. Early examples were the Classics Illustrated versions of H G Wells' The Time Machine and The War Of The Worlds. He soon developed an undying interest in "speculative fiction" and began to write fiction for his own consumption at an early age.
His career took in a wide variety of roles including working in the Agricultural sector and in various laboratories in the worlds of heavy industry and organic chemicals. His longest period of employment was working as a statistician in the Government Statistical Office, concentrating mainly in Balance of Payments issues.
Throughout his time he has remained a passionate advocate for the value of rationality and science in human affairs, one which he sees as of paramount importance in the increasingly turbulent times in which we live.
His works to date are all in the realm of speculative fiction and have received critical acclaim amongst those who love stories which probe the bounds of possibility.

PRAISE FOR THE AUTHOR

Quantum Exile

'A clever blend of science fiction and science fact. The pace of this read is fantastic and the morally grey protagonist is really fleshed out, I both loved and loathed him in different scenarios which just made him all the more human. Vaughan clearly has a good grasp of the quantum mechanics and physics mentioned and applies it perfectly to the worlds (or rather probabilities) he has created within this books universe. I highly recommend this book to any sci fi reader. It truly is difficult to put down!'

Emma Harley – Amazon reviewer

Devouring Darkness

'Chilling, poignant, haunting, and thoroughly gripping. Darkness, intrigue, and ambiguity mark Vaughan's deeply immersive latest, a collection of science-fiction stories…Vaughan's storytelling is immersive as he digs deeper into a complex world and multi-faceted characters, offering life-and-death maneuvering, deadly conspiracies, and looming catastrophe via swiftly unravelling plots. This is a stunner.'

The Prairies Book Review

'These stories are sinister and dark. Martyn's imagination is amazing. The world he has created in these short stories is much appreciated…Go ahead with this book without thinking twice.'

Kia's Reviews, Goodreads

Hideous Night

'Reading this brilliant novel was just like riding a scary roller coaster! I found myself hanging on with an enjoyable sense of dread throughout the many thrilling plot twists and turns, as I the reader was propelled along with each new page towards what seemed like an unavoidably hideous climax. However, I needed to know what happened next so I devoured the book like the hungry monsters that are the villains of this extraordinary story! This thoroughly entertaining book has reminded me how much fun reading good sci-fi can be and I will certainly be ordering the rest of Martyn Rhys Vaughan's back catalogue in the hope of experiencing similar thrilling adventures. In the meantime I will be reflecting on the writer's astute observations of the privilege of modern lifestyle choices and how flawed people can choose to be heroes when forced to fight seemingly overwhelming odds to save (a perhaps undeserving) humanity.'

Wayne Edwards – Amazon Reviewer

Doom Of Stars

'Doom of Stars written by the author Martyn Rhys Vaughan is a SciFi thriller. It is a riveting story with a power to hook the readers from the first page…World building is amazing. I appreciate the author's imagination in creating it…There are lots of things that readers could take away from this novel. Pace of the story is fast and you won't get a chance to feel bored. So, go ahead with it without thinking twice.'

Blogspresso Reviewer

'So much happens in this book, but it does not have that overcrowded or rushed feel to it. We get the whole scope and view of events without the drawn out, lengthy series many SciFis turn into. In the story we follow Kalli, a young woman living in a small village just outside of London, who, along with her fellow villagers, hunts seals and trades goods in London to survive an Earth with sweltering summers, frozen winters, and out of control tides. Her grandmother is legendary, a renowned scientist whose name has become akin to a curse. She brought about these end times, the Doom of Stars. Or did she?
There's something so refreshing and wonderful about the idea of humanity fighting to survive without the

influence of money and wealth or debt. Watching people who have been cut down the bare basics use their skills to find food and survive, working to learn new skills to better their survival, is wholly entertaining. It's a reset button many desperately want.

On top of that, the story is full of strong, incredible, and intelligent women. It skips the usual tropes you see with strong female characters. They have believable insecurities, they aren't infallible or perfect, and they aren't described as being some version of a perfect dream girl. There's barely any emphasis on looks for the purpose of driving their personality. These women feel human and real.

If you enjoy SciFi with real feeling science (I say this as I'm no scientist and couldn't tell you if there's anything real to it or not), great female characters, and the end of the world, definitely give this a read. You won't be disappointed.'

Chelsea Hauth – Reedsy Reviewer

Resolution of Stars

'After reading Martyn Vaughan's Doom of Stars, I was excited to get my hands on its sequel. Resolution of Stars is a captivating story that has the power to hook the reader's attention from the first page itself. Maya is a scientist and so is Professor DeGroot. Maya is unaware of what happened to Earth since the destroyer passed. To Maya, it seems they have discovered a colony of the Burrowers! Read this story to know how Maya's path will cross with the Karn.

The story kept me on edge the whole time as I was curious to know what challenges are ahead. Those who love reading post-apocalyptic stories should definitely get their hands on this one. I appreciate the backdrop setting. It pulled me totally into the story and I forgot the real world around me while reading this book. Language used in the book is medium so I would like to recommend this book to avid readers. Martyn has shared great knowledge about quantum physics. It's an insightful read and you won't be disappointed at all.'

Ankita – Goodreads Reviewer

I keep switching the rating of this book from 5 to 4 to 5 again, changing my opinion with each chapter I finished. It has so many wise things to say about propaganda, grief, trauma and healing. It touches and breaks my heart every time, like very few books do. A great ending to the trilogy! I loved that the story kept moving and things kept happening. There wasn't any "downtime" in the story while waiting for something big to happen.

Let's face it, a series is only as good as its last book. Is a kitchen towel drenched in my tears a good indicator of the quality of Culmination of Stars? I think it is, considering that I am not a crying-over-books type. I think this book is a FANTASTIC ending of a FANTASTIC series. The book is lying next to me now, so deceitful in appearance, with its innocent, bright, cheerful cover. Culmination of Stars is indeed a book which takes you to a very disturbing but very real place. Vaughan is a genius, he is fearless and I have a great respect for the gutsiness of his that didn't allow him to settle for an ending all wrapped up in pink paper with a perfect little bow. I am sure he knew that the faint of heart would be enraged. But he stuck to his guns and stayed true to his message and to his characters.

Also, I will be falling short of word limit since have so much to tell you guys about the beauty of this book keeping aside the story and the plot. But I will say this: It was non-stop action. From the very first page there was something going on and I loved it. I'm so glad I was able to read straight through because I don't think I would have been capable of putting it down. It's thought provoking and emotional. While Culmination of Stars gave me answers, it's also left me thinking about what I read, days after I finished the book. This book burned. It's radiant!!

Oshin Rathore – Goodreads Reviewer

I highly recommend "A Culmination of Stars: The Stars Trilogy Book 3" by Martyn Rhys Vaughan.
Wow! This final installation is an incredible read and just like this author's other novels did not disappoint. However, I recommend finishing books one and two of the trilogy before embarking on this epic journey. This is due to the fact that what makes this such a masterpiece is how the information, characters, and events from the previous books are built upon in this third of the trilogy. Creating it in this fashion allows the characters and plot to continue to develop in a meaningful way that left me reaching for the next page with bated breath.
Spoiler alert! In the second book, I was introduced to a group of massive Lightsail ships. These special crafts are filled with the world's brightest crew and hundreds of select individuals personally selected for fertilization and work ethic to continue the human race and man the ships themselves. At the end of book 2, the Lightsail ships have taken off into space at more than half of the speed of light to reach the Centauri solar system in search of a habitable planet where they can start anew.
This third and final book of the trilogy starts right where book two left off and was an epic adventure beyond my greatest imagination. I was seamlessly taken

back and forth through centuries to build upon the characters that were introduced in the previous books. The first two installations have a single female protagonist but this incredible novel has several and includes everything from humans with downloaded minds to powerful beings from outer space.

Once again the use of descriptive words and imagery is excellent and helped me to create a picture of each scene in the book. For example, one moment I was in a meeting drinking an interesting invention of cyrocoffee, and the next flying with attached wings through the air at great speed. I could taste the bitter brew and feel the air on my face as I flew high above the ground.

I give this five stars out of five and recommend this to 9th graders and above due to the expansive vocabulary present.

Pick all three books from this trilogy and hang on tight as you are about to take off and endure an amazing edge-of-your-seat science fiction trip that is quite literally out of this world!

Jessica Rainstein – Amazon Reviewer

ALSO BY MARTYN RHYS VAUGHAN

The "Stars Trilogy":
Doom of Stars: ISBN 978-1-8382805-6-7
Resolution of Stars: ISBN 978-0-9574894-4-8
Culmination of Stars: ISBN 978-0-9934886-9-6

The Vampire Novels:
No Truce With The Vampires: Those Who Sleep
            ISBN: 978-1-3999-8905-3
No Truce With The Vampires: Those Who Wake
            ISBN: 978-1-0369-0304-6

Quantum Exile: ISBN 978-1-9161619-6-2
The Cave Of Shadows: ISBN 978-1-9161619-9-3
Hideous Night: ISBN 978-1-8380752-2-4
Devouring Darkness: ISBN 978-1-8384289-5-2

Follow Martyn Vaughan's Science Fiction Work on
Facebook, Instagram, Pinterest and Goodreads.